P9-APX-606

3⁰⁰

TONY HILLERMAN
THE WAILING WIND

"ONE OF HILLERMAN'S BEST . . .
This is a satisfying mystery whose ending you'll be
hard-pressed to figure out ahead of time . . . It's also
a bit of a love story . . . Any way you look at it, *The
Wailing Wind* is a good read, and it leaves you waiting
for the next Hillerman mystery. But then, they all do."
Denver Post

"HILLERMAN EXCELS . . .
His Leaphorn/Chee mysteries [are] more than
just ordinary police procedurals . . . What he
communicates better than almost any other suspense
writer is a different sense of time, a different sense of
connection to nature, a different way of being. His
portrait here of people and places haunted by greed
but blessed by beauty is deeply affecting."
Ft. Worth Star-Telegram

"TONY HILLERMAN STRIKES IT RICH
WITH *THE WAILING WIND*,
as Jim Chee and Joe Leaphorn investigate
murders old and new. With its deft mixture of
legend and atmosphere, the book is vintage
Hillerman . . . No fool's gold here. Hillerman's
fans will treasure this tale."
Orlando Sentinel

Also by Tony Hillerman

TONY HILLERMAN

THE WAILING WIND

HarperCollins*Publishers*Ltd

First paperback edition

National Library of Canada Cataloguing in Publication

Hillerman, Tony
The wailing wind / Tony Hillerman.

ISBN 0-00-639210-5

I. Title.

PS3558.I45W34 2003   813'.54   C2002-904676-9

HCNY 9 8 7 6 5 4 3 2 1

Printed and bound in the United States

AUTHOR'S NOTE

While *The Wailing Wind* is fiction, the Fort Wingate Army Ordnance Depot is real. It sprawls over forty square miles east of Gallup adjoining transcontinental rail lines, old Highway 66 and Interstate 40, causing generations of passing tourists to wonder about the miles of immense bunkers. These once sheltered thousands of tons of bombs, rockets, and missiles, but now they are mostly empty. Antelope graze along abandoned railroad sidings—as do a few buffalo left over from a breeding experiment and the cattle of neighboring ranchers, some of whom are accused of cutting

AUTHOR'S NOTE

fences to facilitate this. TPL, Inc., is at work in some of the bunkers converting rocket fuel into plastic explosives, and Paul Bryan, Brenda Winter, and Jim Chee of that company earned my thanks by helping me with this project.

The fort began in 1850, moved to its present site in 1862. It became a depot for immense amounts of military explosives at the end of World War I, grew with World War II and the Korean War, and became the principal depot for explosives used in Vietnam. Now decommissioned, it is occasionally used by the army to fire target missiles over its White Sands anti-aircraft base, and a few bunkers and other buildings are occupied by government offices.

My old friend James Peshlakai, Navajo shaman, singer of important curing rituals, and director of the Peshlakai Cultural Foundation, has allowed me to use his name for the fictional shaman of Coyote Canyon, and my thanks also go to Lori Megan Gallagher and to Teresa Hicks for helping me research mining legends.

THE WAILING WIND

The Wailing Wind

Illustrated by Laura Hartman Maestro ©2002

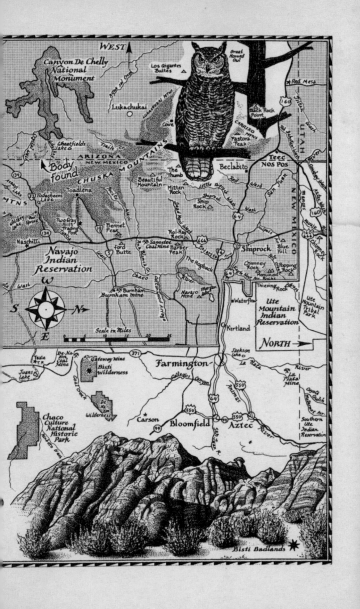

ONE

OFFICER BERNADETTE MANUELITO had been having a busy day, enjoying most of it, and no longer feeling like the greenest rookie of the Navajo Tribal Police. She had served the warrant to Desmond Nakai at the Cudai Chapter House, following her policy of getting the most unpleasant jobs out of the way first. Nakai had actually been at the chapter house, obviating the hunt for him she'd expected, and—contrary to predictions of Captain Largo—he had been pleasant about it.

She had dropped down to the Beclabito Day School to investigate a reported break-in there. That was nothing much. A temp maintenance employee had overdone his weekend drinking, couldn't wait until Monday to get a jacket he'd left behind, broke a window, climbed in and retrieved it. He agreed to pay for the damages. The dispatcher then contacted her and canceled her long drive to the Sweetwater Chapter House. That made Red Valley next on her list of stops.

"And Bernie," the dispatcher said, "when you're done at Red Valley, here's another one for you. Fellow called in and said there's a vehicle abandoned up a gulch off that dirt road that runs over to the Cove school. Pale-blue king-cab pickup truck. Check the plates. We'll see if it's stolen."

"Why didn't you get the license number from the guy reporting it?"

Because, the dispatcher explained, the report was from an El Paso Natural Gas pilot who had noticed it while flying yesterday afternoon and again this morning. Too high to read the plates.

"But not too high to tell it was abandoned?"

"Come on, Bernie," the dispatcher said. "Who leaves a car parked in an arroyo overnight unless he stole it for a joyride?" With that he gave her a little better description of the probable location and said he was sorry to be loading her up.

"Sure," said Bernie, "and I'm sorry I sounded so grouchy." The dispatcher was Rudolph Nez, an old-timer who had been the first to accept her, a female, as a fellow cop. A real friend, and she had a feeling he was parceling her out more work to show her he looked on her as a full-fledged officer. Besides, this new assignment gave her a reason to drive up to Roof Butte, about as close as you could drive to ten thousand feet on the Navajo Reservation. The abandoned truck could wait while she took her break there.

She sat on a sandstone slab in a mixed growth of aspen and spruce, eating her sack lunch, thinking of Sergeant Jim Chee, and facing north to take advantage of the view. Pastora Peak and the Carrizo Mountains blocked off the Colorado Rockies, and the Lukachukai Forest around her closed off Utah's peaks. But an infinity of New Mexico's empty corner spread below her, and to the left lay the northern half of Arizona. This immensity, dappled with cloud shadows and punctuated with assorted mountain peaks, was enough to lift the human spirit. At least it did for Bernie. So did remembering the day when she was a brand-new rookie recruit in the Navajo Tribal Police and Jim Chee had stopped here to show her his favorite view of the Navajo Nation. That day a thunderstorm was building its cloud towers over Chaco Mesa miles to the northeast and another was taking shape near Tsoodzil, the Turquoise Mountain of the East. But the rolling grassland below them was bright under the afternoon sun. Chee had pointed to a little gray column of dirt and debris moving erratically over the fields across Highway 66. "Dust devil," she had said, and it was then she had her first glimpse behind Chee's police badge.

"Dust devil," he repeated, thoughtfully. "Yes. We have the same idea. I was taught to see in those nasty little twisters the Hard Flint Boys struggling with the Wind Children. The good *yei* bringing us cool breezes and pushing the rain over grazing land. The bad *yei* putting evil into the wind."

She finished her thermos of coffee, trying to decide what to do about Chee. If anything. She still hadn't come to any conclusions, but her mother seemed to have deemed him acceptable. "This Mr. Chee," she'd said. "I heard he's born to the Slow Talking Dineh, and his daddy was a Bitter Water." That remark had come apropos of absolutely nothing, and her mother hadn't expanded on it. Nor did she need to. It meant her mother had been asking around, and had satisfied herself that since Bernie was born to the Ashjjhi Dineh, and for Bead People, none of the Navajo incest taboos were at risk if Bernie smiled at Chee. Smiling was as far as it had gone, and maybe as far as she wanted it to go. Jim Chee was proving hard to understand.

But she was still thinking about him when she pulled her patrol car up the third little wash north of Cove and saw the sun glinting off the back window of a truck—pale blue as described and blocking the narrow track up the bottom of the dry wash.

New Mexico plates. Bernie jotted down the numbers. She stepped out of her car, walked up the wash, noticing the vehicle's windows were open. And stopped. A rifle was in the rack across the back window. Who would walk off and leave that to be stolen?

"Hello," Bernie shouted, and waited.

"Hey. Anyone home?" And waited again.

No answer. She unsnapped the flap on her

holster, touched the butt of the pistol, and moved silently to the passenger-side door.

A man wearing jeans and a jean jacket was lying on his side on the front seat, head against the driver-side door, a red gimme cap covering most of his face, knees drawn up a little.

Sleeping one off, thought Bernie, who'd been in police work now long enough to recognize that. But she didn't detect the sick odor of whiskey sleep. No sign of motion. No sign of breathing, either.

She sucked in a deep breath, moved a fraction closer to the door. "*Ya eeh teh,*" Bernie said, loudly. No answer. She could see no sign of blood or any hint of violence. Strands of the man's long, curly blonde hair were visible around the cap. His jean jacket and shoes were dusty. It seemed to Officer Manuelito he was emphatically unconscious if not dead. She opened the door, grabbed the door post, pulled herself up on the running board. She pushed up the bottom of the jean-clad leg and reached for his ankle to check for a pulse. The ankle was cold. No pulse, and as cold as death.

The feel of the lifeless ankle under her hand

abruptly replaced in Bernie's mind her awareness of herself as cop with an awareness of
herself as Navajo. A thousand years before the
Dineh were aware of bacteria or viruses, they
were aware of the contagion spread by the
newly dead and the dying. The elders called
this danger *chindi*, the name of a ghost, and
taught their people to avoid it for four days—
longer if the death came inside a closed house
where the *chindi* would linger. Bernie stepped
off the running board and stood for a moment.
What should she do now? First she would call
this in. When she got home, she would ask her
mother to recommend the right shaman to
arrange the proper curing ceremony.

Back at her patrol car she gave the dispatcher her report.

"Natural, you think?" he asked. "No decapi-
tation. No blood. No bullet holes. No smell of
gunpowder. Nothing interesting?"

"It looked like he just died," Bernie said.
"One bottle too many."

"Then I've got an ambulance over at
Toadlena, if it's still there. Hold on a minute
and I'll let you know."

Bernie held on. The hand holding the mike
was dirty, smeared with what looked like soot.

From the dead man's shoe, she guessed, or his pant leg. She grimaced, switched the mike to her left hand, and wiped the dirt away on the leg of her uniform trousers.

"Okay, Bernie. Got him. He should be there in less than an hour."

That proved to be overly optimistic. An hour and almost twenty-two minutes had plodded past before the ambulance and its crew arrived, and to Bernie it seemed a lot longer. She sat in her car thinking of the corpse and who he might have been. Then got out and scouted around the pickup to reassure herself she hadn't overlooked anything—such as a row of bullet holes through the windshield, or a pool of dried blood on the floor around the brake pedal, or bloodstains on the steering wheel, or maybe on the rifle in the window rack, or a suicide note clutched in the victim's hand.

She found nothing like that, but she noticed that the victim's jeans had collected lots of those troublesome chamisa seeds in their travels, and so had the sock on the ankle she had tested—chamisa seeds, sandburs, and other of those stickery, clinging seeds by which dry-country plants spread their species. The rubber sole of the sneaker on the foot she'd touched had also accumulated five goathead stickers—the curse of bike riders. She sat in her car, considering that, and climbed out again to inspect the local flora. Here it was above nine thousand feet, not the climate for chamisa. She found none now, nor any sandburs or goatheads. She collected the seedpods from a cluster of asters, gone to seed early at this high, cold altitude, and which just possibly might grow in the hotter climate of her Shiprock flower bed. She added the seeds from two growths of columbine and from a vine she couldn't identify. And being tidy, she went back to the columbines and salvaged the little Prince Albert pipe tobacco tin she'd noticed among the weeds. It was dirty, but it was better than trying to carry her seed collection loose in her pocket.

TWO

JOE LEAPHORN had been slow to learn how to cope with retirement, but he had learned. And one of the lessons had been to prepare himself when he tagged along with Professor Louisa Bourbonette on one of her excursions. These tended to be out to the less acculturated districts of the Navajo reservations to collect memories of elders on her "oral history" tapes. That usually left him sitting in an oven-hot hogan or lolling in her car and had caused him to buy himself a comfortable folding chair to relax upon in the shade of hogan brush arbors.

He was relaxing in it now under a tree beside the hay barn of the Two Grey Hills Trading Post. The breeze was blowing out of cumulus clouds forming a towering line over the ridge of the Lukachukai and producing an occasional promising rumble of thunder. Louisa was selecting a rug from the famous stock of the Two Grey Hills store—a wedding gift for one of Louisa's various nieces. Since the professor took even grocery shopping seriously, and this was a very special gift, Leaphorn knew he had plenty of quiet thinking time. He had been thinking of Louisa's quest for perfection amid the Two Grey Hills rug stock as sort of a race with the thunderhead climbing over the mountain. Would the rain come before the purchase? Would both purchase and cloud fizzle without success—the cloud drifting away to disappointing dissipation in dry air over the buffalo plains and Louisa emerging from the T.P. without a rug? Or would the cloud climb higher, higher, higher, its bottom turning blue-black and its top glittering with ice crystals, and the blessed rain begin speckling the packed dirt of the Two Grey Hills parking lot, and Louisa, happily holding the perfect collectors'-quality rug, signaling him to drive over to the porch to keep the raindrops from hitting it.

A dazzling lightning bolt connected the slope of the mountain with the cloud, producing an explosive crack of thunder and suggesting the cloud might be winning. Just then a Chevy sedan rolled into the parking lot, with SHERIFF painted on its side. The driver slowed to park near the porch, then aborted that move and rolled his car over to Leaphorn's tree.

"Lieutenant Leaphorn," said the driver, "you oughtn't be sitting under a tree in a lightning storm."

A face from the past. Deputy Sheriff Delo Bellman.

Leaphorn raised his hand in greeting, considered saying: "Hello, Delo," but said: "Delo, *ya eeh teh.*"

"You been listening to the news?" Delo asked.

"Some of it," Leaphorn said. Bellman didn't need a radio to collect the news. He was widely known as the premier gossip of the Four Corners Country law enforcement fraternity.

"Hear about the killing?" Bellman said. "That man your guys found dead near Cove the other day. It turns out he was old Bart Hegarty's nephew. Fellow named Thomas Doherty."

Leaphorn produced the facial expression appropriate for such sad news. His experiences with Bart Hegarty had been neither frequent nor particularly pleasant. He hadn't been among the mourners when the sheriff hadn't survived sliding his car into an icy bridge's abutment a few winters back. "Died of what?" Leaphorn asked. "If he was the sheriff's nephew he must have been fairly young."

"Late twenties, I guess. Bullet in the back," said Bellman, with the somber pleasure gossips feel when passing along the unpleasant. "Rifle bullet."

That surprised Leaphorn, pretty well saying the Doherty boy hadn't been shot in the car. But he didn't ask for details. He nodded, trying not to give Bellman an interested audience. Maybe he would go about his business. Leaphorn had heard on the TV news last night that neither cause of death nor identity of the victim had been released by the FBI. But the mere fact the Federals had taken the case away from the NTP had told Leaphorn that either it was a homicide or the victim was a fugitive felon.

Bellman chuckled. "Funny, don't you think? A woman named Hegarty would marry a man named Doherty." He glanced at Leaphorn, awaiting a response. Getting none, he said: "You know, an 'arty marrying an 'erty."

"Yeah," Leaphorn said.

"Probably a hunting rifle," Bellman added, and waited for a comment from Leaphorn. "Looked like whoever done it was quite a ways behind Doherty. Just took a bead on him and went bang." Leaphorn nodded. So the crime scene crew had concluded the victim had been shot, and then put in the vehicle where he was found. Interesting.

"That's probably why your officer had it pegged as natural causes, no sign of violence."

"Did he?"

"She," Bellman said. "It was the Manuelito girl."

Bernadette Manuelito, Leaphorn was thinking. Smart young woman, from the impression he'd had of her last year when he'd gotten involved with Jim Chee in investigating that casino robbery business. Smart, but she'd still be a greenhorn. "Well," he said. "Things like that are hard to see sometimes, and I think she's new at patrolling. I can understand how she could miss it."

Easy to understand, he thought. Bernie was the daughter of a traditional Navajo family, taught to respect the dead and to fear death's contamination—the *chindi* spirit that would have lingered with the body. She wouldn't have wanted to handle it. Or even be around it more than she could help. Just turn the body over to the ambulance crew and keep her distance.

"I hear the Feds aren't so understanding. Heard they bitched to Captain Largo about the way she handled it." Bellman chuckled. "Or didn't handle it."

"What brings you to Two Grey Hills?" Leaphorn asked, wanting to change the subject and maybe get Bellman moving. It didn't work.

"Just touching bases," Bellman said. "Finding out what's going on." He restarted his engine, then leaned out the window again.

"I'll bet the FBI is going to give Jim Chee a ration of paperwork out of this. You think?"

"Who knows?" Leaphorn said, even though he knew all too well.

Bellman grinned, knowing Leaphorn knew the answer, and recited it anyway. It had three parts. The first was the friction between Sergeant Chee and the Federal Bureau of Investigation, widely known and happily celebrated in the Four Corners Country law enforcement fraternity; the second being a general belief by the same fraternity that Captain Largo, where the buck stopped in the Shiprock district of the Navajo police, detested paperwork and would pass it down where Sergeant Chee would be stuck with it; the third being gossip that Chee and Officer Manuelito had romantic inclinations—which meant Chee would strain himself to defend her from any allegations of mishandling evidence in a homicide.

"And something else, Joe," Bellman continued, "I got a feeling you're going to get interested in this one before it's over."

Leaphorn opened his mouth, closed it. He wanted Bellman to drive away before Louisa came out with her trophy, or without it, rushing up and giving Bellman more ammunition for his gossip mill. "Guess who I saw with old Joe Leaphorn out at the T.G.H. trading post?" Bellman would be saying. But now Leaphorn was curious. He blurted out a "Why?"

"The stuff they found in Doherty's truck. Bunch of maps, some computer printouts about geology and mineralogy, a whole bunch of Polaroid photographs taken in canyons, that sort of material."

Leaphorn didn't comment.

"Had a folder full of reprints of articles about the Golden Calf Mine," Bellman added. "I'll bet that will remind you of old Wiley Denton and what's his name? The con man Wiley killed five years ago. McKay, wasn't it?"

"Marvin McKay," Leaphorn said. Yes, it did remind him, but he wished it hadn't. The Wiley Denton case was one he'd like to forget if he could. And he probably could, if he could ever find out what had happened to Wiley Denton's wife.

THREE

SERGEANT JIM CHEE came out the side exit of the Navajo Tribal Police headquarters in a mood compatible with the weather—which was bad. The gusting west wind slammed the door behind him, saving Chee the trouble, blew up the legs of his uniform pants, and peppered his shins with hard-blown sand. To make things worse, the anger he was feeling was as much against himself—for complicating the problem—as against the Chief for not just telling the FBI to mind its own business and against Captain Largo for not handling this himself.

Part of the dust blown against Chee was

now being stirred up by a civilian pickup
truck being parked in one of the clearly
marked "Police Vehicle Only" spaces. It was a
familiar truck, blue and banged up, rust spot
on the right fender—the truck of Joe Leaphorn, now retired but still the Legendary Lieutenant.

Chee took two steps toward the truck and
was abruptly beset by the familiar mixed feelings of irritation, admiration, and personal in-
competence he always had around his former
boss. He stopped, but Leaphorn had his window down and was waving to him.

"Jim," he shouted. "What brings you down
to Window Rock?"

"Just a little administrative problem," Chee
said. "How about you? Here at the office, I
mean?"

"I was just scouting around for somebody to
buy me lunch," Leaphorn said.

They got a table at the Navajo Inn, ordered
coffee. Chee would eat a hamburger with fries
as always, but he pretended to study the
menu while struggling with his pride. All during the long drive down U.S. 666 from his
Shiprock office in answer to the Chief's sum-
mons, he'd considered going by Leaphorn's

place and asking for some advice. This idea had been rejected on various grounds—unfair to bother the lieutenant in his retirement, or he should be able to deal with it himself, or it would make him look like a nerd in the eyes of his former boss, or. . . . Finally he'd rejected the idea—and then there was Leaphorn waving at him through the dust.

He glanced over the menu at Leaphorn, whose own menu still lay unopened on the table.

"I always have an enchilada," Leaphorn said. "People fall into habits when they get older."

That seemed to Chee as good an opening as any. "You still have that habit of being interested in odd cases?"

Leaphorn smiled. "I hope you mean the killing of that Doherty boy. I'm sort of interested in that."

"What do you hear?" Chee asked, thinking it would be just about everything—except maybe the final twist to his own problem.

"What I read in the *Gallup Independent* and the *Navajo Times*, which was what the FBI was telling. No suspect. And I guess no known motive. Doherty apparently shot somewhere else, hauled to where he was found in his own pickup truck. That's about it."

"How about what's on the rumor circuit?"

"Well, it's said that the FBI's not happy with how the crime scene was handled." Leaphorn was grinning at him. "And if I was into betting, I'd bet that's what brought you down to see the Chief today."

"You'd win," Chee said. "The dispatcher sent Officer Manuelito out to check on an abandoned truck. Bernie looks in and sees the body. Doherty slumped over on the driver's side. No blood. No sign of violence. Just like ten thousand drunks you've seen pulled over to sleep it off. When Doherty doesn't wake up, Bernadette reaches in to check an ankle for a pulse. It's cold. So then she calls in and asks for an ambulance and hangs around waiting for it."

Chee stopped. Leaphorn waited. He sipped his coffee.

Chee sighed. "And she says she walked around some, collecting seed pods and that sort of thing. Bernie's a botany buff. The ambulance guys pull the body out and then, finally, the blood gets noticed. Of course by that time everybody has walked all over everything. But there wasn't a way in the world Bernie could—" He stopped. With Leaphorn, there was never any need to explain anything.

He waited for Leaphorn to tell him that Bernie should have looked more closely at the situation, should have taped off the site. But of course Leaphorn didn't. He just sipped a little more of his coffee and put down his cup.

"I ran into Delo Bellman yesterday at Two Grey Hills. He said Doherty had a bunch of stuff with him relating to gold mining. Some articles about that famous old Golden Calf diggings. He said it would remind me of the Wiley Denton case. Wiley shooting that con man. That sound right?"

Chee nodded, made a wry face. "As you may have heard I'm not all that popular with the Bureau these days. But the grapevine told me it looked like Doherty might have been looking into that McKay homicide himself. I heard some of the stuff the Federals found in his briefcase must have been copied out of the evidence files in that homicide."

"He was old Bart Hegarty's nephew," Leaphorn said. "And it's an old dead case. He could have gotten that easily enough."

"I gather there's no suspect yet. I wonder if

the Bureau has picked Denton as its man," Chee said.

Leaphorn sipped his coffee and considered. Chee was asking him what he thought about that idea. And, indeed, the fact was he had thought about it. He hadn't found any sign of a sensible connection, but something about it nagged at him. Hinted there might be one if he was smart enough to find it.

"What would be Denton's motive?" Leaphorn asked.

"Pretty vague," Chee said. "I guess the theory of the crime is that Doherty wanted to finish what McKay started. Tell Denton he'd located the Golden Calf, try to milk him for some money."

Leaphorn smiled. "Vague indeed," he said. "That would make him either pretty stupid. Or maybe suicidal." He wanted off this subject. To get Chee to tell him what was really on his mind. So he said: "Bellman said he heard the Federals wanted Manuelito suspended."

"That seems to be true," Chee said.

Leaphorn shook his head. "I wouldn't worry much about it. Nothing happens if you arrest the killer. Otherwise if a scapegoat is required, she'd get suspended a week or so.

Probably with pay. I'd think that would be the worst."

Chee said: "Well . . . ," then stopped.

Leaphorn waited awhile, took another sip of coffee. "Miss Manuelito seemed like a fine officer from what I saw of her when you were working on that casino robbery. Probably has a good record in her personnel jacket. But maybe there's something I don't know about this."

"There is," Chee said. "Can I talk to you in confidence? Because I may wish I'd kept my mouth shut."

Their lunches arrived. Leaphorn stirred sugar into his fresh cup of coffee.

"I guess you're sort of asking if maybe you can tell me something that if it came down to crunch I might have to deny you told me?"

"Something like that," Chee said. You never had to explain anything to the Legendary Lieutenant.

"Well," Leaphorn said. "I think I know you well enough so I can rely on your judgment. Go ahead and tell me."

Chee extracted a Ziploc bag from his jacket pocket and put it on the table.

"Officer Manuelito picked this up at the

crime scene, in a bush beside the car. She used it to hold the weed seeds she'd been collecting."

"Looks like an old Prince Albert tobacco tin," Leaphorn said.

He looked at Chee, expression curious.

Chee took another plastic bag from his pocket, handed it to Leaphorn.

"When she got home and dumped her seeds out into a bowl, this came out."

"Looks like arroyo bottom sand," Leaphorn said. He shook the bag in his palm, studied it. "Or is it?" he asked. "Color's a little off and it seems too heavy."

"It's partly sand and I think it's partly placer gold dust."

"Be damned," said Leaphorn. He opened the plastic bag, rubbed a pinch of the sand between his fingertips, and examined what stuck to the skin. "I'm no assayer, but I'll bet you're right."

"She said she picked up the can from some weeds maybe three or four feet from the driver-side door," Chee said. "Gave it to me because she thought it might be evidence." He laughed at that, a sort of grim laugh.

"For you to give to the FBI?"

"Sure," Chee said, sounding bitter. "To do my duty. And absolutely guarantee she'll get suspended with a reprimand in her file. I told her that's what would happen, and she said she guessed she deserved it." Chee grimaced at that and looked down into his cup, seeing not coffee but Bernie standing rigidly in front of his desk, looking very small, very slim, her black hair glossy and her uniform neater than usual. She had glanced down and away, made one of those vague motions with her lips that expressed regret and apology and then looked up at him, her dark eyes sad, awaiting his verdict. And he had understood then why he'd never rated her as cute. There was dignity in her face. She was beautiful. And then she had said: "I guess I'm just too careless to be in police work." And what had he said? Something stupid, he was sure. And now Leaphorn was studying him, wondering why he was just staring into his cup of coffee.

"It might be evidence, all right," Leaphorn said. "With that placer gold in it. It could be connected to the crime."

"So, Lieutenant, how do I handle this? I guess I'm asking you what you'd do if you were me."

Leaphorn put a forkful of enchilada in his mouth. Chewed it. Took another bite. Frowned. "Do you know the L.C. of this one? Is it the one you got crosswise with a couple of years back in that case involving the eagle poaching?"

"No. He was transferred," Chee said. "Thank God for that small favor."

Leaphorn took another bite, said: "But the memory will linger in the federal tribe for a while."

"I'm sure it will," Chee said.

"I think if it was me, and the officer was a good one I wanted to keep in my department, I'd take that tobacco can and put it back exactly where Bernie found it. Then I'd tell someone, in a suitably subtle way, someone who had some business out there, tell them where to look for it and ask him to go find it. Then he could call the FBI and tell them he's noticed this tin out there and let them find it for themselves. Do you have any of your Shiprock people working the crime scene?"

"They've dealt us out of it," Chee said. He'd thought he'd got beyond being surprised by Leaphorn, but he hadn't. Was the Legendary Lieutenant volunteering to do this himself?

Leaphorn was smiling, mostly to himself.

"Well then, I've got a legitimate reason to go out there and take a look," he said. "I still get kidded now and then about being obsessed with that McKay killing. I'll be looking for a connection. Worst they can do is tell me to go away."

"Connection? Isn't that going to sound pretty weak?"

"Awful weak," Leaphorn said. "Maybe I'll just tell 'em I'm a bored old ex-cop looking for a way to kill time. Maybe they'll be finished at the scene and nobody will even ask."

"I've always wondered why you were so interested in that case," Chee said. "Hell, Denton laid it all out. Admitted he shot McKay, claimed it was self-defense, and worked out a plea bargain. You've had doubts about that?"

"He got a year, served part of it with time off for behaving," Leaphorn said. "I had some doubts about the self-defense, but mostly I've always wondered what happened to Linda Denton."

"Linda Denton? What do you mean?" Leaphorn was surprising him again. Chee checked his memory. The way it came to him, the young Mrs. Denton had set her wealthy old hubby up for McKay's swindle and then ran when the plan didn't work out. "Now I'm wondering why you've been wondering."

Leaphorn smiled, consumed a bit more of his lunch. Shook his head.

"You're going to think I'm an old-fashioned romantic," he said. "That's what Louisa—what Professor Bourbonette says. Tells me to get real."

Chee finally took the first bite from his hamburger, studying Leaphorn. The Legendary Lieutenant actually looked slightly abashed. Or was he imagining it?

"You really want to hear all this?" Leaphorn asked. "It takes time."

"I do," Chee said.

"Well, of course it was a McKinley County case because Denton built his house outside Gallup city limits. Lorenzo Perez was undersheriff then and handling major crime investigations. Good man, Lorenzo. He had himself a clear-cut uncomplicated case with the shooter admitting it. Only question was how much self-defense was involved. Where'd the gun come from the con man had? You remember the story Denton told? McKay had told him he'd located the Golden Calf diggings and needed money to file claims and begin development. He'd let Denton in for fifty grand. In cash. So Denton drew the money out of his bank, had it in a briefcase at his house. McKay shows him a bunch of stuff, a little bit of placer gold, part of a map, some other stuff. Denton spots it as bogus, tells McKay to get out. McKay says he'll take the money with him. He pulls a gun and Denton shoots him."

Leaphorn stopped. "McKay was an ex-con with a record of trying to run con games. That didn't seem to leave much to investigate."

"Yeah," Chee said. "That's the way I remember it. But how does this bring us to Linda Denton? The story was she wasn't home when it happened."

"Denton said she'd gone to have lunch with some friends and wasn't there when it happened and never did come back. He said he was worried. Couldn't imagine what had happened to her." Leaphorn made a wry face. "It seemed pretty easy to guess if you remember the circumstances. Turned out Linda had introduced McKay to her husband. Denton said she'd met McKay before she married him. Met him at that bar-grill where she used to wait tables."

Their waiter came and refilled their cups. Leaphorn picked his up, looked at it, returned it to the saucer. "And she never did come back. Ever. Not a word. Not a trace."

It sounded sad, the way he said it, and Chee asked: "Didn't that seem natural? Young gal working in a bar meets a rich guy about thirty years older, bags him, then decides he's too boring for her taste so she locks onto a slick-talking young con man to get the old bird's money. It turns into a homicide with her maybe facing some sort of conspiracy charge. So she runs."

"That's the way I read it at first," Leaphorn said. "Lorenzo wanted to find her. See what she had to say. I started on it. Went out to see her folks at Thoreau. Couple named Verbiscar. They were frantic. Said she would never leave Denton. Loved him. Something had to have happened to her."

Chee nodded. It seemed to him about the sort of response you'd expect from the woman's parents. And he noticed Leaphorn had sensed his attitude.

"They sat me down and told me her story," Leaphorn said. "Great kid. Went to the St. Bonaventure School there. Real bookish girl and very much into music. Not much for boyfriends. Good grades. Scholarship offers from University of Arizona, couple of other places. But her dad had a heart problem. So Linda Verbiscar turned the scholarship down and enrolled at the U.N.M. branch at Gallup. She got herself that restaurant waitress job. She and another girl from Thoreau rented themselves a little place out on Railroad Avenue. Brought home a boyfriend once for them to look over but decided he was sort of stupid. Then she brought Wiley Denton out to meet them."

Leaphorn paused, the polite Navajo gesture to give the listener a chance to comment.

Chee tried to think of something sensible to say, and came up with: "Linda doesn't sound like the kind of woman I had in mind."

Leaphorn nodded.

"They said it scared 'em to death when she showed up with Wiley Denton. She was twenty then and he was early fifties. Older than her dad, in fact. Big, homely, rich old guy." Leaphorn chuckled. "Verbiscar said they knew he hadn't been born rich because he had the kind of broken nose that can't be overlooked and is easy to fix if you can pay the surgeon. All they really knew about him was he had been in the Green Berets in the Vietnam War, made a ton of money off oil and gas leases out around the Jicarilla Reservation and built himself that huge house on the slope outside Gallup. That, and everybody said he was an eccentric sort of loner."

Leaphorn stopped again, drank coffee. Looked over the cup at Chee. "Did you ever meet him?"

"Denton? No. I just saw him on television a time or two. At the sentencing, I guess. I just remember thinking if they had charged him with being ugly he was guilty."

"Well, Mrs. Verbiscar said they got invited to a meal at his house and the big impression he made on her was that he was bashful. She said she noticed he had a grand piano in the living room and asked him if he played and he said no, he'd bought that for Linda to play if he could get her to marry him. She said he seemed real shy. Sort of clumsy. Nothing much to say."

Chee laughed. "What some people would call 'deficient in social graces.'"

"I guess," Leaphorn said. "He seemed that

way to me when I interviewed him with Lorenzo Perez. But to get on with this, both of Linda's parents said they liked him. Way too old for their daughter, but she seemed to love him dearly. And a little after she turned twenty-one she said she wanted to marry him. And she did. Catholic wedding. Flower girls, ushers, the whole business."

"Now the bad part starts," Chee said. "Am I right?"

Leaphorn shook his head. "Unless a lot of people were lying to me that didn't start until the day Denton killed the swindler. But I was thinking like you are. When she went missing, I went to talk to people who knew her."

Leaphorn's first call had been on the woman Linda Verbiscar had lived with in Gallup. Linda and Denton were a match made in heaven, she'd said. Linda didn't date much. Uneasy with men. Sex would wait until she met the right man, and married him, and then it would be forever. But something about Denton, homely as he was, attracted her right away. And awkward and bashful as he was, you saw it was mutual.

"According to her roommate, Miss Verbiscar seemed to like the awkward and bashful types," Leaphorn said, and chuckled. "And broken noses. The only other man she seemed real friendly with was a Navajo. Couldn't remember his name, but she remembered the crooked nose. She said Linda never went out with him, but he'd come in the place middle of afternoons when it was quiet. He'd get a doughnut or something and Linda would sit down and talk to him. Nothing going there, but with Denton it got to be real, genuine, romantic love."

Leaphorn paused with that, looked thoughtful. "Or, so her roommate said."

"Okay," said Chee. "Maybe I've been too cynical."

And then Leaphorn had gone to Denton's massive riverside house and talked to his housekeeper and his foreman. It was the same story, with a variation—the variation being that now Denton was falling deeply in love. Obsessively in love, the housekeeper had said, because Mr. Denton was an extremely focused man who tended to be obsessive. His overpowering obsession had been to find that legendary mine. Which was what the housekeeper and the foreman said got him into the trouble with McKay. But the bottom line was, there was no way they would believe the official police theory. Linda would never, never leave Wiley Denton. Something had happened to her. Something bad. The police should stop screwing around and find her.

While Leaphorn talked, Chee finished his hamburger, and his coffee, and another cup. The waiter left his ticket and disappeared. The gusty wind rattled sand against the window where they sat. And finally Leaphorn sighed.

"I talk too damn much. Blame it on being retired, sitting around the house with nobody to listen to me. But I wanted you to see why I think there was more to that killing than we knew."

"I can see that," Chee said. "Any chance they thought Denton might have figured Linda had sold him out? Bumped her off in the famous jealous rage?"

"I asked 'em both. They said she'd left to go downtown to have lunch with some lady friends that morning. Usual huggy-kissy goodbye at the car with Wiley. Then about middle of the afternoon Denton had asked if she had called. He was wondering why she was late. Held up dinner for her. Then McKay showed up. The help told Perez they'd heard McKay and Denton talking in the den, and then the talking got loud, and then they heard the shot."

Leaphorn paused, looking for comment.

"Does that match what you were told?"

"Just the same," Leaphorn said. "They said after the shot, Denton came rushing out and told them to call nine one one. Said McKay had tried to rob him. Pulled a pistol on him so he'd shot McKay and he thought he'd probably killed him."

"So Linda never came home?"

"Never got to the luncheon with her lady friends, in fact," Leaphorn said. "And when they booked Denton into the Gallup jail and he called his lawyer, he told the lawyer he was worried about her. See if he could find her. Let him know."

"Sounds persuasive," Chee said.

"Then after Denton bonded out, he hired a private investigators outfit in Albuquerque to find her. Next, when he went away to do his prison time, he had advertisements placed in papers here and there, asking her to come home."

This surprised Chee. This wasn't the sort of

information the Legendary Lieutenant could have obtained casually on the cop grapevine. Interest there would have died with the confession. Leaphorn obviously maintained his interest. He'd made this something personal.

"Placed advertisements from the federal prison?"

"Easy enough. Just had his house manager do it."

"Saying what?"

"In the *Arizona Republic* it was a little box ad in the personals. Said 'Linda, I love you. Please come home.' About the same in the *Gallup Independent*, and the *Farmington Times*, and the *Albuquerque Journal*, and the *Deseret News* in Salt Lake. Then he ran some more offering a twenty-thousand-dollar reward for information about her whereabouts."

"Never a word?"

"I guess not."

This also surprised Chee. It seemed out of character.

"You talked to him about it?"

"I tried to after he came home from prison," Leaphorn admitted. "He called me a son of a bitch and hung up."

FOUR

OFFICER BERNIE MANUELITO had risen even earlier than usual, driven over to her mother's place at Hogback, had a most unsatisfactory visit, went on to Farmington thinking she would use this unexpected (and undeserved) day off to shop, decided that was a bad idea considering the mood she was in, and headed south on Route 371 to the Tsale Trading Post. She'd have a talk with old man Rodney Yellow. Hostiin Yellow was her mother's senior brother, the elder male in the Yoo'l Dineh—the Bead People clan—and a shaman. He had been very active in the Medicine Man Association and in the movement to train young singers to keep some of the less-used curing rituals alive. More important to Bernie, he had conducted the *kinaalda* ceremony for her when she reached puberty, had given her her secret ceremonial "war name," and was her very favorite uncle.

Hostiin Yellow was also an authority on what the scientists out at the Chaco National Monument called "ethnobotany." Maybe he could tell her something about the various stickers and seedpods she'd found on the victim's pant legs and socks. Which was why, she told herself, she was going to visit him. That and family duty. She glanced down at the speedometer. Eleven miles over the limit. Oh, well. Never any traffic on 371. The emptiness was one of the reasons she loved to drive it. That and passing the grotesque monuments of erosion of the Bisti Badlands, and seeing the serene shape of the Turquoise Mountain rising to the east. Pretty soon now it would be wearing its winter snowcap, and monsoon rains of late summer had already started turning the grazing country a pale green. Enjoying that, she forgot for a moment how arrogant Sergeant Chee had acted, but the memory of it came right back again.

"And just keep your mouth shut about it,"
Chee had said, giving her his stern "I'm your
boss" look. He had taken the tobacco tin from
her hand, put it in a plastic evidence sack,
and placed the sack in his shirt jacket pocket,
and said: "I'll see what I can do about this," and
walked into Captain Largo's office. When he
came out he gave her another of those looks
and told her to go home, take the rest of the
week off, and: "For God's sake, don't talk to
anybody about this."

That was it. He didn't even have the de-
cency, the respect, to tell her she was suspended. Maybe she wasn't. Just take the rest
of the week off, he said—looking very dour.
Big deal. That was just a day and a half before
her shift ended anyway. What had Largo said
after Chee told him about the tobacco tin?
The captain had already been angry after his
meeting with the FBI guys. Not that he
chewed her out much. Just asked a bunch of
questions. And glared at her. But then he
hadn't known about her taking the tin away—
a tin that Chee seemed to think would have
had prints on it. Hers now, if none other.

Hostiin Yellow wasn't at his place behind
the Tsale Trading Post. The lady there said he

was supposed to be doing his botanical talk for the kids at the Standing Rock School. Bernie took the dirt road shortcut thirteen miles over the mesa and saved about thirty minutes by driving too fast. She caught him coming out of a classroom, trailed by a swarm of middle-school kids, and steered him into the room reserved as a faculty lounge. There they went through the ritual of family concern and affection. But she could tell Hostiin Yellow had sensed instantly that this was not a casual "drop in on the way" visit.

He put the big cardboard box holding his collection of botanical and mineral specimens on the table, sat himself in one of the folding chairs, and eyed her curiously while she completed her recitation of family news.

And finally she said: "And how about you? You look tired."

And he said: "Girl Who Laughs, stop chattering now and tell me your trouble."

Thinking about it later, she decided hearing her war name spoken did it—broke through her dignity and reduced her from woman to niece. Hostiin Yellow had given her that secret name—to be revealed to no one outside the bosom of her family. It was the name of

her sacred identity and used only in dealing
with the Holy People. If it became known to
witches, it could be used against her.

She sat in the chair he pointed her to, dug
out a tissue to deal with the unwelcome tears,
and told him everything. Of finding Doherty's
body curled in the cab of his truck; of possibly
losing her job because she hadn't handled it
right; of taking away the old tobacco tin,
which turned out to have tiny bits of placer
gold mixed with the sand in it, and how that
was getting her into trouble with everybody;
of her mother being unsympathetic and
telling her she never should have gone into
police work. Her mother saying this trouble
was good, maybe it would bring her to her
senses. And when she told her mother how
curt Sergeant Jim Chee had been, she had
taken Chee's side. Called him a good man.
Said Bernie should start treating him better.

When the lightning storms ended and the
Season When the Thunder Sleeps made it
possible, she would ask him to do for her the
proper sing to protect her from ghost sickness.

Finally, with that said, Girl Who Laughs became Officer Bernadette Manuelito again,

and she got to the reason she thought she had come to look for him, knowing now it was just a cover story—just an excuse.

She took an envelope from a pocket and poured its contents onto the tabletop. Hostiin Yellow looked at the little litter of seedpods and burrs, and up at her.

"When I reached in to see if the victim had a pulse, to see if he was still alive, I noticed his socks and his trouser legs had picked up all sorts of stickers," Bernie said. "Chamisa seeds, for example, but no chamisa grows way up there where we found his truck. The same with some of these other seeds, so I thought maybe they had come from where he was when he was shot."

Hostiin Yellow had reached up and extracted a pencil from his *tsiiyeel*, using the bun in which traditional Navajos wear their hair as a holder. Now he was using the pencil tip to sort Bernie's botanical material into separate bunches.

"I thought maybe you could help me find where it came from," Bernie said. But even as she said it, she knew it was an impossible job. The stuff she'd collected could have grown just about anywhere that was hotter and drier than the Chuska Mountain high-country zone. About anywhere in the millions of acres of tundra from which the mountains rose.

"Chamisa seed," said Hostiin Yellow, inspecting the fragment held between thumb and finger. "Chamisa needs some salt. In the old days, before people could buy salt blocks for their sheep, they used to have to drive them down out of the mountains to the *halbatah*—the 'gray lands' where the salt-holding plants grow. No salt in the high country soil. The runoff from the melting snow leaches it out."

He glanced at Bernie. She nodded. She knew all this. Hostiin Yellow had taught her as a child.

"If there are no salty plants, sheep start eating the stuff that poisons them." He held up another seed. "This sacatan grass grows down in the Halgai, in the flatlands. There used to be plenty of it everywhere. Good food for the animals, but they bite it off right down to the roots. So pretty soon it's crowded out by this." He held up silvery needle-grass seeds. "Not even goats will eat this unless they're starving."

Hostiin Yellow finished his descriptive in-

ventory without seeming to Bernie to add anything that would help pin down the location of
the source.

"You think all of these came from the same
place? Why do you think that?"

"Well," Bernie said. "Not a very good reason, I guess. Jim Chee said there was a new
Zip Lube oil-change sticker on the windshield
and the sales slip in the glovebox. It showed
he had the oil changed the morning he was
killed and he'd driven only ninety-three miles
from the station in Gallup. And from the Zip
Lube place to the truck it was thirty-five miles.
So that leaves fifty-eight miles to get to where
his socks collected the stickers and from that
place to where we found him."

"That's the shortest way from Gallup? The
thirty-five miles?"

Bernie nodded. "North out of Gallup on six
sixty-six, then northwest to Nakaibito, and
then up that gravel road past the Tohatchi
lookout, and on toward Cove."

"So," said Hostiin Yellow, "this poor fellow
collected his stickers quite a ways from where
you found him. Down the mountain. East side
or west side. Either New Mexico stickers or
Arizona stickers."

He stared past her, out the window, looking at the mountains, lost in thought.

"Was this all you got? Any other seeds you didn't bring with you?"

Bernie shook her head. "Well," she said, "I noticed a bunch of those goathead stickers in the soles of his sneakers."

"Goatheads? You mean the puncturevine, I think. Dark green, spreads very close to the ground. Seeds usually have three long sharp thorns?"

She nodded.

Hostiin Yellow frowned. "That doesn't fit well with the chamisa and the spikeweed and the other plants," he said. "Puncturevine likes more water, loose soil. Gets crowded out where there's too much heat."

He leaned back, stuck the pencil back into his bun. "You know, I think this man must have been walking up some sort of drainage, an arroyo, or a narrow canyon, where the puncturevine would have some damp sand and some shade. You know anything that might fit that idea?"

That thought interested Bernie. Placer mining required runoff water, didn't it? And sand, of course. There was sand in the Prince Albert tin. The one Chee had ordered her to keep her mouth shut about.

"I found an old tobacco tin not far from the body. The sand in it had a little bit of gold dust mixed in it."

"Gold dust, was it? I think . . ." He stopped, studying her. "How bad do you need to find this place? Can't you just let the other cops do it?"

I need to find it to save my dignity, she thought. To restore my self-respect. To show those jerks I'm not a dummy.

"Pretty bad," Bernie said. "I need to save my job."

Hostiin Yellow was pushing the piles of her seeds into a single heap, returning them to her sack. He said: "I need to say something to you about this gold. Gold has always brought trouble for the Dineh. It makes the *belagaana* crazy. General Carlton thought we had a lot of gold in our mountains, so he had the army round up us Navajos and move us away on that long walk to Bosque Redondo. They drove the Utes out of Colorado to get the gold in their mountains. And drove the tribes out of the Black Hills, and pretty much killed the

California Indians. Everywhere they find gold, they destroy everything for it. They tear up our Mother the Earth, they break the cycle of life for everything."

Bernie nodded.

He handed her the sack. "It makes people crazy," he said. "And crazy people are dangerous. They kill each other for gold."

"My uncle," Bernie said. "I think you are telling me Mr. Doherty was murdered because of that gold. And I think you know where he got all those stickers in his pants. Can you just tell me?"

He shook his head. "I'll think about it," he said. "Right now, I think you should let the other policemen find that place."

Bernie nodded. But she could tell from his expression that he didn't interpret that gesture as consent. She sat and watched him.

And Hostiin Yellow watched her. As hunter for the white men, his Girl Who Laughs had lost her laughter. Why must she care who had done this crime? If a *belagaana* did it, let the *belagaana* punish him if they must. If it was a Navajo—one who still lived by Changing Woman's laws—then he would come to be cured of the dark wind that had caused him to kill. But no good to tell this young woman all this. She knew it. And Girl Who Laughs would live her life her own way. That, too, was Navajo. He was proud of that, too. And of her.

She was glancing away from him now, at something outside the window. Her face reminded him of the old photograph in the museum at Window Rock—the women who had endured their captivity at Bosque Redondo. The narrow, straight nose, the high cheekbones, the strong chin. None of the roundness here that the gene pool of the Zuñis, Hopis, and Jemez had contributed to the Dineh. Beauty, yes. Dignity, too. But nothing soft about Girl Who Laughs.

Hostiin Yellow sighed.

"Girl Who Laughs, you have always been stubborn. But I want you to listen to me now," he said. "The *belagaana* have always killed for gold. You already know that. You have seen it. But have you thought about how some people kill for religion?"

Bernie considered that, looking for a connection and seeing none. Hostiin Yellow was studying her.

"Are you hearing what I say?"

Bernie nodded again. "Yes," she said. But she really wasn't. "You mean like the Israelis and the Palestinians? And the people in the Balkans, and . . ."

Hostiin Yellow's expression told her he was disappointed.

"Like people in Ganado or Shiprock or Burnt Water or Albuquerque or Alabama or anywhere," he said. "When the wind inside turns dark and tells them it must be done."

Bernie tried for an expression that would suggest she understood. It didn't seem to work.

"You have seen what the coal mining has done to our Earth Mother on Black Mesa. And other places. Have you seen what these modern placer mines do? Great jets of water washing away everything. The beauty is gone. Our sisters the plants, our brothers the animals, they're all dead or washed away. Only the ugly mud is left."

"I saw a documentary about that high water-pressure placer mining. On public television. It made me sad. And then it made me angry," Bernie said.

"Think and consider," Hostiin Yellow said. "If it makes you angry, it might make some people angry enough to kill. Think about it. What if those are the people you are looking for? What do they do if you find them?"

FIVE

LEAPHORN STOPPED his pickup beside a patrol car bearing the decal of the Apache County Sheriff's Department, which told him the scene of the Doherty homicide was officially decided to be in Arizona and not in San Juan County, New Mexico, a few feet to the east. The car was empty. Fifty feet beyond it, fenced off behind a yellow crime scene tape, was Doherty's blue king-cab truck with a burly fellow in a deputy uniform sitting on its tailgate looking at Leaphorn.

Who did he know in the Apache County department? The sheriff, of course, an old-timer, and the undersheriff, but neither of those would be out here. Once Leaphorn had known all the deputies, but deputies come and go, changing jobs, getting married, moving away. Now he knew fewer than half of them. But he could see he knew this one, who was walking toward him. It was Albert Dashee, a Hopi Indian better known as Cowboy. And he was grinning at Leaphorn.

"Lieutenant," Deputy Dashee said. "What brings you up here to the scene of our crime? I hope you're going to tell me that New Mexico admitted the Arizona border is actually over there"—Dashee pointed to the west side of the arroyo—"and San Juan County has to do the baby-sitting for the Federals instead of me."

"No," Leaphorn said. "I was just feeling curious about this homicide. I thought I'd come up and see if I could take a look."

"I can think of two reasons you might be curious," Dashee said, still grinning.

"Two?"

"One is the Bureau blaming Jim Chee's girlfriend for messing up the scene. And one is the Bureau looking for a way to connect this with Wiley Denton killing that con man.

Killing McKay. You were always interested in that one."

"Let's just say I'm like an old retired fireman who can't stay away when something's burning." He was thinking how impossible it was to keep a secret, maintain even a shred of privacy, in the small world of police work. "You're looking well, Cowboy," he said. "I haven't seen you since that Ute Mountain casino robbery business."

Their chat lasted maybe five minutes, and then Leaphorn walked to the tape, looked at the truck, and said: "Found the body in the front seat. That right?"

"Curled up on the seat cushion," Dashee said. "Head against the driver-side door, feet the other way. Like sleeping. Hell, I'd have figured it just like Bernie did. Another drunk." He held the tape down so Leaphorn could step easily over it. "In case anybody asks, I said you can't come in without permission from the agent in charge."

Leaphorn peered through the window, touching nothing. He looked in the truck bed, through the small side window into the passenger cab. Crouched to examine the tire treads and to look under the vehicle with Cowboy trailing along, watching him and talking.

"Oops," Cowboy said. "I hear my radio," and he was trotting away to his car.

Leaphorn slipped the tobacco tin from its sack and pushed it into a secluded and weedy corner. That done, he circled the truck, examining the maze of tracks left by ambulance people and the swarm of investigators who followed.

Then Cowboy was back.

"They're sending a tow for the truck," Cowboy said, moving back toward the tape. "You finished here? Seen anything interesting?"

"Not much," Leaphorn said. "I guess you noticed that tobacco tin over there by the brush." He pointed. "I thought maybe it might have fallen out of the truck when the medics were taking the body out. Then it could have got kicked over there."

Dashee examined Leaphorn a moment. "Where?"

Leaphorn walked over. Pointed.

Dashee squatted, peered, looked up at Leaphorn, nodded, and straightened up.

"Funny the crime scene crew didn't notice

that," he said, looking at Leaphorn. "Don't you think?"

Leaphorn shrugged. "City boys, those agents," Leaphorn said. "Lawyers, accountants. Very good at what they're good at. How good would we be working a mail fraud case in Washington?"

Dashee was rewarding Leaphorn with a broad grin tinged with skepticism and directing him back over the crime scene tape, back toward Leaphorn's pickup, opening the door for him.

Leaphorn got in, started the engine, then turned it off.

"You said the Bureau was connecting this case with Wiley Denton killing the con man. Do they think Doherty was trying to work some sort of swindle like McKay?"

"The Federals don't confide much in us sheriff deputies," Dashee said.

"But they talk to the deputy's boss when they have to and sheriffs like to share the information."

Dashee grinned. "I've heard a couple of agents were at Fort Wingate following Doherty's tracks, and they found out he was very interested in the archives out there. And they found Wiley Denton's telephone number in Doherty's notebook."

Denton's number. Leaphorn's eyebrows raised.

"Really? If my memory is good from five years ago, Denton had an unlisted number."

"He still does," Dashee said.

Leaphorn let this new information digest for a moment.

"And those archives he was looking into. The Navajo Nation's?" The Navajo Nation had been using one of the multitude of explosives bunkers at the old fort to store its old records and documents. But why would Doherty have an interest in those? None Leaphorn could think of.

"No," Cowboy said. "He was checking into the old fort archives. Especially records going back to the 1860s. When the prospectors were making all those fabulous gold discoveries, and coming in wanting the fort to protect them from us savage and hostile redskins."

Interesting, Leaphorn thought. "I guess you have to sign in to get access. Is that how they knew he was looking?"

"Better than that," Dashee said. "They even

knew what pages he looked at. Found his fingerprints."

"On old paper?"

"I didn't believe it either. But Osborne—"
Dashee stopped. "I didn't say his name. He
ain't supposed to be telling stuff like this to a
civilian cop. But anyway Special Agent John
Doe was telling me about a technique they
use now that picks up the fingerprint oil off of
all sorts of rough surfaces. On smooth surfaces, like glass or metal, it evaporates after a
day or two. On cloth or paper it absorbs. He
said they even recovered the fingerprints off
cloth wrappings of one of those Egyptian
mummies."

Leaphorn was checking his memory rela-
tive to the Prince Albert can. Had he been
careful enough? Probably. But how about
Chee? And how about Officer Bernie Manuelito?

He heard the diesel sound of the tow truck
coming to haul Doherty's king cab off to
where it could be given the fine-tooth-comb
laboratory treatment. He restarted his engine, waved at Dashee, and headed home.
Fort Wingate, he was thinking. So Doherty's

path toward sudden death had taken him there. Had McKay's fatal journey also involved a stop at the obsolete old fort? His own futile hunt for the young and beautiful Mrs. Wiley Denton had taken him there. He would pull out his old file and see if the notes he'd made on that frustrating visit to the fort would tell him anything.

SIX

As ALWAYS, Leaphorn awoke at middawn before the edge of the sun rose over the horizon. It was a Navajo hogan habit, dying out now, he presumed, as fewer and fewer of the Dineh slept in their bedrolls on hogan floors, went to bed early because of lack of electric lighting, and rose with the sun not only for the pious custom of greeting Dawn Boy with a prayer but because hogans were crowded and tradition made stepping over a sleeping form very bad manners.

Normally Leaphorn spent a few minutes waking up slowly, watching the sunlight turn the high clouds over the mountains their various shades of pink, rose, and red, and remembering Emma—who had suggested in her gentle way that their first view of the day should be of the sun's arrival just as Changing Woman had taught. This was another Leaphorn habit—awakening with Emma on his mind. Before her death he'd always reached over to touch her.

For months after her funeral, he continued that. But touching only her pillow—reaching for the woman he loved and feeling only the cold vacuum her absence had left—always started his day with grief. He'd finally dealt with that by switching to her side of the bed so this habitual exploration would take his hand to the windowsill. But he still came awake with Emma on his mind, and this morning he was thinking that Emma would approve of what he intended to do today. He intended to see if he could find some way to get a handle on what had happened to pretty little Linda Denton.

He was in the kitchen, having toast and his first cup of coffee, when Professor Louisa Bourbonette emerged from the guest bedroom wrapped in her bulky terry-cloth bathrobe, said, "Good morning, Joe," and walked past him to the coffeepot.

"Way past midnight when I got in," she added, suppressing a yawn. "I hope I didn't wake you."

"No," Leaphorn said. "I'm glad you made it. Wanted to ask you if you know anything about a spooky Hispanic legend about La Llorana. Which I probably mispronounced."

"You did," said Professor Bourbonette. She was eyeing the file folder open beside his plate. "It's a tale told about a lost woman, or about a lost woman with a lost child whose sorrowful cries can be heard at night. There are several versions, but the authorities pretty well agree they all originated in the Valley of Mexico and then spread north into this part of the world."

She nodded toward the file. "That looks official," she said. "I hope it's not."

"It's just some personal notes I kept on that old McKay homicide. The case was closed right away. You may remember it. Wiley Denton confessed he shot the man. Claimed self-defense. McKay had a criminal record as a swindler, and Denton got a short term."

Louisa sat across the table from him and sipped her coffee.

"That the one in which the shooter's wife sort of simultaneously disappeared? Did she ever come back?"

Leaphorn shook his head.

"You surprise me," she said. "I've been reading about that Doherty homicide in the Flagstaff paper. I thought you might be getting interested in that."

"Well, there might be a connection."

Louisa had looked very sleepy while pouring her coffee. Now she looked very interested. She was a small, sturdy woman with her gray hair cut short, holding a tenured position on the Northern Arizona University anthropology faculty with, to her credit, a long list of publications on the legends and oral histories of Southwestern Indian tribes and the old settlers who invaded their territory. And now she was smiling at Leaphorn, expectantly.

"A connection," she said. "Does it connect to the Legend of the Wailing Woman or just to Gallup's richest man shooting his swindler?"

"Probably neither," Leaphorn said. "It's very shaky, very foggy." But as he said that he knew he would tell her about it, discuss it with this white woman. With that knowledge came the familiar guilty feeling. This had been one of the ten thousand reasons he'd loved Emma—this business of laying the problems and troubles of his work before her and finding as he talked, as he measured her reactions, the fog tended to lift and new ideas emerge.

He shouldn't share with another woman this special link he'd had with Emma. But he had done it before with Louisa—a sign of his weakness. And so he turned his notebook to a blank page, got out his pen, and began drawing.

Louisa laughed. "A map," she said. "Why did I know there would be a map?"

Leaphorn found himself grinning. It was a habit he was often kidded about. The dominant feature on the wall in his Criminal Investigation Division office at Navajo Tribal Police headquarters had been an enlarged version of the Indian Country map of the American Automobile Association—a map defaced with hundreds of pinheads, their colors identifying incidents, events, or individuals whom Leaphorn considered significant. The black pins represented places where Navajo Wolves had been reported being seen or where complaints of other witchcraft activities of these mythical "skinwalkers" had been registered. The red ones marked homes of known boot-leggers, blue ones dope dealers, white ones cattle thieves, and so forth. Some were foot-noted in the precise and tiny script he used, others coded with symbols only Lieutenant Leaphorn understood. Everyone in the law-and-order community seemed to know of this map, and of the smaller versions Leaphorn kept in his vehicle—mapping out whatever case he happened to be working on at the time.

"I can't deny it," Leaphorn said. "I admit I like maps. They help me sort out my thinking. And on this map, here's Wiley Denton's man-sion, where he shot McKay. The straight line is Interstate Forty and the railroad running into Gallup. And over here . . ." He drew a large rectangle. "Here is Fort Wingate." He created more squares, circles, and symbols and used the pen as a pointer, identifying them.

"Gallup," he said. "And over here's where Doherty's body was found, and this is Mc-Gaffey School."

Louisa examined the sketch. "Lots of big empty blank spaces," she said. "And you haven't told me what McGaffey School has to do with any of this. And where's your mark for the Wailing Woman?"

Leaphorn tapped a spot on the edge of his Fort Wingate square closest to the McGaffey square. "I think that should be about here," he said.

Louisa looked surprised. "Really? I hope you're going to explain this now."

"Maybe not," Leaphorn said. "I'm afraid you might take it seriously."

"I won't," she said, but her expression denied that.

"Think of it in terms of connections," Leaphorn said. "There seem to be three, with one of them very fuzzy." He held up one finger. "Two shooting victims. Both had collected information on that legendary lost Golden Calf mine. McKay seemed to have claimed he'd found it. Doherty seemed to be looking for it. McKay goes to meet Denton and Denton shoots him. Doherty had Denton's unlisted telephone number written in his notebook."

Leaphorn paused.

Louisa nodded, held up one finger, said: "One connection."

Leaphorn held up two fingers.

"Doherty did some of his research out at the Fort Wingate archives. Probably McKay did, too. Natural enough, because in those days when prospecting was booming, the fort was the only military base out here. It was supposed to provide them protection from us Indians."

Louisa frowned. "Yes. Seems natural they would. But that doesn't seem to mean much. What are you looking for?"

Leaphorn then held up three fingers—one of them bent.

"Now we come to the vague and foggy one. When Denton shot McKay it was Halloween evening." He stopped, shook his head. "I'm sort of embarrassed to even mention this."

"Go ahead. Halloween gets my attention."

"The McKinley County sheriff's department had two calls that evening. One was the Denton shooting McKay business out here." Leaphorn pointed to Denton's house on the map. "And the other was a call from McGaffey reporting a woman screaming and wailing out on the east side of Fort Wingate."

"Oh," said Louisa. "The Wailing Woman legend comes into play at last. Right?"

"Not quite yet." Leaphorn said. "And maybe

we should call it the Wailing Wind legend. Question of what, or who, was doing the wailing. Anyway the sheriff sent a deputy out and called Fort Wingate security people. They scouted around and couldn't find anything and decided it was just some sort of Halloween prank."

"So how do we get to the Wailing Woman legend?"

"Months later," Leaphorn said. "Denton had started doing his time in that federal white-collar prison in Texas and he began running ads in the *Gallup Independent*, *Farmington Times*, and so forth. Personal ads, addressed to Linda, and signed Wiley, saying he loved her and asking her to come home. I asked around, learned that Linda Denton hadn't been around since the killing. That seemed odd. I checked. Never reported missing, except her parents had talked to the sheriff about it—thinking something must have happened to her."

"No wonder," Louisa said. "What happened next?"

"Nothing," Leaphorn said. "She was a mature married woman. No mystery to the killing. Denton did it. Confessed he did it.

Worked out a plea bargain. Dead case. The official theory was that Mrs. Denton had been working with McKay and when the deal went sour and he got shot, she just took off. No crime. No reason to look for her."

"But you did."

"Well, not exactly. I was just curious."

"So am I," Louisa said. "About when you're going to tell me about how this old Hispanic legend of the tragedy of a lost lady got involved in this gold mine swindle."

"I heard about that Halloween evening call, got the name of the caller, and went out to see her. She's a teacher out at McGaffey School. Said these kids showed up at her house that Halloween night—students of hers. They told her about cutting across the corner of the fort to get out to the road and catch a ride into Gallup, and they heard these awful terrifying moans and crying sounds. She said they seemed genuinely frightened. She'd called the sheriff."

"And his deputy found absolutely nothing?"

Leaphorn chuckled. "Nothing. But she told me it turned out to have a healthy benefit because two of the kids were Hispanics, who connected the sounds with the Wailing Woman ghost story, and one was a Zuñi. She thought they were hearing a skinwalker, or another of the Navajo version of witches, or maybe that Zuñi spirit who punishes evildoers, and the white girl thought it might be an ogre, or vampire, or one of their things. So the word spread around McGaffey School, and it put an end to the student body's practice of taking that forbidden shortcut."

"Did you talk to any of the kids?"

"Somebody from the sheriff's office did."

"You didn't."

"Not yet," Leaphorn said. He picked up the old notebook, flipped through it.

"I still have the names. You want to go with me?"

"Golly," she said. "I wish I could. I've got to meet with an old man named Beno out at Nakaibito. He's supposed to know a story about his great-grandmother being captured by the Mexicans when she was a child. His daughter is bringing him into the trading post there to talk to me. Could it wait?"

"It could," Leaphorn said. "But it's already waited a long, long time."

SEVEN

THE FIRST NAME on Leaphorn's old list was a Zuñi girl whose father worked at Fort Wingate and who was now a student at the University of New Mexico and out of reach. The second was Tomas Garcia, now a husband and father. Leaphorn found him at his job with a Gallup lumber company.

Garcia threw the last bundle of asphalt shingles on the customer's flatbed truck, turned up his shirt collar against the dusty wind, and grinned at Leaphorn. "Sure, I remember it," he said. "It was a big deal, getting interviewed by a deputy sheriff when you're in high school. But I don't think it ever amounted to anything. At least not that any of us ever heard about."

"You mind going over it again? They didn't put much in his report."

"There wasn't much to put," Garcia said. "I guess you know the layout at Wingate. Miles and miles of those huge old bunkers with dirt roads running down the rows. It's easy to get through that fence the army put up in the olden days when it was storing ammunition out there, and we'd cut through there to get to the highway when we wanted to go into Gallup. That evening one of the kids was having a sort of Halloween party in town. So we were going to that. Catch a ride in, you know. Cutting across through the bunkers, we started hearing this wailing sound."

Garcia paused, recalling it, bracing himself against the west wind that was blowing dust around their ankles. "I guess it was just the Halloween idea in our heads. Kids, you know. But it was spooky. Just getting real dark, and a cold wind blowing. At first I thought it was the wind, whistling around those bunkers. But it wasn't that."

"What do you think it was?"

He shook his head. "Why don't we talk

about this where it's warm," he said. "Get Gracella in on it, too. She might remember it better than I do."

"Is that Gracella deBaca?" If it was, Leaphorn had found the fourth person on his list.

"Gracella Garcia now," Garcia said, looking proud of that.

Leaphorn followed Garcia's pickup home and got a free lunch of excellent *posole* generously seasoned with pork. Gracella was on maternity leave from her job at the McKinley County hospital, and to Leaphorn's unpracticed eye she seemed extremely close to motherhood. Her account of that twilight Halloween was much like her husband's—as Leaphorn had expected. They would have relived the affair and more or less agreed on the memory.

"It was very, very scary," Gracella said, as she dished Leaphorn another dipper of *posole*. "Tomas pretends he thinks it was just some sort of a practical joke for Halloween. That's what the cops told us." She gave her husband a stern look. "But he knows better," she said. "He's just macho. Doesn't want to admit he believes in La Llorona."

Garcia let that pass. They'd been over this before.

"I'm not saying it wasn't Gracella's mythical lost mother, but how about the music?"

"We always get to that," Gracella said. "I'm not even sure I heard the music. Maybe you talked me into that."

"What sort of music?"

"Not my kind," Garcia said. "I'm into hard rock, or heavy metal. This sounded like classical stuff."

"You could barely hear it," Gracella said. "The wind was blowing. Sometimes you thought you heard like a piano playing. Sometimes not."

"The wailing and the music came together?" Leaphorn asked.

"I better explain," Garcia said. "We were hurrying along, cutting across where the rows of bunkers are lined up. And we heard a scream. Or sort of like a scream from a long ways off. So we stopped and tried to listen. And we heard it again. Plainer this time. More like wailing." He glanced at Gracella. "Right?"

She nodded.

"So we stopped and just stood there awhile," she said. "We heard it some more. And we decided to turn around and go back and report it to the police. While we were talking about that, the wailing stopped. And then after a while we heard the piano music. Tomas thought that proved it was just Lloyd Yazzie trying to scare people. Playing a recording, you know?"

"Why Lloyd Yazzie?"

"He was a guy in the band," she said. "And the music sounded like a piece we practiced. A real jerk."

After that, nothing. The wind had risen. They walked back to McGaffey and got the teacher to call the sheriff.

"What do you think was causing it?" Leaphorn asked.

They looked at each other. "Well," Gracella said. "Nobody has proved there aren't any ghosts."

Garcia laughed, which irritated Gracella.

"Okay," she said. "You can laugh. But remember that one deputy didn't laugh. He thought it was serious, and he came back to talk to us later."

Garcia's expression dismissed that. "That was old Lorenzo Perez," he said. "That was after Mr. Denton was in jail and started running those advertisements asking his wife to come home. Lorenzo thought Mr. Denton had got jealous and killed her, and he was running those advertisements to make himself look innocent."

"I don't care," Gracella said. "Anyway, he didn't act like he thought it was just a joke."

The last name on Leaphorn's list seemed to have vanished with time—apparently part of the nomadic movement of *belagaana* families who follow jobs around the country. He spent the rest of the afternoon taking a look at part of the 130 square miles that make up what was, when Leaphorn was a lot younger, the Fort Wingate Army Ordnance Depot, finding the approximate place where the Garcias had their fright, and trying to imagine what might have been happening to cause it. When Leaphorn had driven past this place on U.S. 66 as a very young man, it had been busy. Its bunkers, built for World War II, had been full of the shells and gunpowder of the Vietnam War. With the end of the Cold War it had been "decommissioned" and had slipped into a sort of semi-ghost town identity. The Navajo Nation stored records in a couple of bunkers; the army used a bit of it on the edge of the Zuñi Mountains to launch target missiles to be shot at by the Star Wars scientists at White Sands

Proving Grounds; other agencies used a bunker here or there for their purposes, and TPL, Inc., had machinery set up in others converting the rocket fuel still stored there to a plastic explosive useful in mining.

What made the old fort interesting to those who persisted in hunting the several legendary gold mines of the adjoining territory was its checkered history. The so-called "fort" had originated about 1850 when the Americans were replacing the Mexicans as landlords of the territory. It was called Ojo del Oso then, after the spring where travelers had stopped and bears came down out of the Zuñi Mountains to get a drink. Next it was called Fort Fauntleroy, honoring a colonel who had served bravely in the Mexican war. But said colonel went south in 1860 to serve bravely in the Confederate Army, causing the name to be changed to Wingate, after an officer free of secessionist loyalties. During the efforts of Carlton to round up the Navajos into the concentration camp at Bosque Redondo and clear the Four Corners mountains for prospectors hunting the gold he coveted, it had been used as a sort of holding pen for Dineh families being herded eastward into captivity.

It played the same role in reverse when President Grant let the tribe go home to their "Dine' Bike'yah," their land between the sacred mountains, in 1868.

The gold prospectors of the time had come often to the fort. They found a little gold here and there, but the huge bonanza discoveries always seemed to be "lost" before they could be exploited. They produced more legends than wealth. As Leaphorn recalled its history, the fort had been expanded from 100 square miles to 130 square miles in 1881 for reasons no one seemed to understand. It had been used as a sort of internment camp for Mexicans fleeing Pancho Villa during the Mexican Revolution, as a center for sheep research, as a vocational school for Indians, etc.; but its major role came as the place where the military could store immense amounts of high explosives that, as Leaphorn's uncle had explained it to him, "wouldn't kill nobody important if they blew away this whole part of the world."

There had been times when the fort was busy, with trains rolling in and out on the network of spur tracks from the main lines and hundreds of employees kept busy with the loading. But on this afternoon, as Leaphorn drove under the rusty iron arch over the main entrance, all was quiet. Two pickups were parked down a side street in front of a warehouse, and a car sat in front of the modest old headquarters building. Leaphorn parked beside it, went up the steps into the office, and looked around. He hadn't been here in years—since the first year he had been called in from Crownpoint and assigned to run the special investigations office in Window Rock. But nothing seemed to have changed.

A gray-haired woman arose from behind the counter, where apparently she had been filing something. She hadn't changed much either—had already been wrinkled and gray last time he'd seen her close up. Teresa Hano was her name. He was amazed that he remembered it.

"Good to see you again, Lieutenant," she said. "You law enforcement people seem to be taking a lot of interest in us all of a sudden. What brings you out here? And in plain clothes, too."

And now he was surprised she remembered him. He laughed, patted his denim jacket, said: "This is what I'm wearing all the time now. No more policeman."

"No?" she said. "I was guessing you're interested in the killing of the Doherty boy. If you were, I couldn't tell you anything much. Nothing I didn't already tell the FBI men."

"Actually I'm more interested in an old Halloween prank—if that's what it was."

Teresa Hano said, "Oh?" and looked puzzled.

"It was the night Mr. Wiley Denton shot that swindler at his house over near Gallup. That same night some kids from McGaffey were cutting across the fort and heard—"

"Yes, Yes," Mrs. Hano said. "And called the sheriff. Lot of excitement over that." The memory produced a happy smile. Excitement must be as rare at a closed-down army base as it was for a retired policeman.

"That wasn't a criminal case, of course," he said. "But I always wondered about it. Four teenagers hearing that crying or wailing and thinking it must be a woman. I know your security folks helped the deputy check around the next day and no one ever found anything.

Has anything interesting turned up since then?"

"Not that I heard of," Mrs. Hano said.

"But since you mentioned the Doherty boy," Leaphorn said, "what was it he wanted to look at in the archives when he was out here?"

"The gold-mining stuff," Mrs. Hano said. She made a wry face. "We don't get many archive customers out here. And they come in two kinds. They're either students working on stuff in history or anthropology. Writing something about the 'Long Walk' you Navajos went on, or about the time we were keeping the Mexican Revolution refugees out here. Or wanting to look at the Matthews papers."

She had pulled open a drawer below the counter, extracted a ledger and flopped it open.

"Are the ethnography professors still going over the Matthews stuff?" Leaphorn asked. He'd done it himself when he was working on his master's thesis at Arizona State. Dr. Washington Matthews had been a surgeon at the fort in the 1880s and '90s, had learned the language and had written report after report on the religion and culture of the Navajos— pretty well laying the groundwork for scholarly studies of the tribe. But by now Leaphorn guessed the anthropologists had pretty well plowed the Matthews papers.

"Washington Matthews," Mrs. Hano said. "Your *hataalii neez*. Your 'tall doctor.' Haven't had any ethnographers rereading his stuff lately, but the gold hunters have discovered him."

"Really," Leaphorn said. "What'd he know about that?"

"Wrote a letter about some of the tall tales the prospectors coming in here were telling back then. I think that's it."

"Was Doherty one of them?"

"I guess indirectly," she said. "What he wanted was to see whatever that McKay fellow looked at. The man Mr. Denton shot."

"Doherty, too? From what I've read there are several reports in these files about the troubles the prospectors were having with us, and the Apaches and the Utes, and what they were reporting about their finds. Would Doherty run across the Matthews stuff looking through that? Sort of on a fishing expedition?"

"I don't think so. I remember him real well because he came in here several times and he'd spend a lot of time reading and I didn't know him and I didn't want him slipping out with anything. But no. The first time he was here he asked about the Matthews letters, and if we had copies of his correspondence with a doctor back in Boston. He had the doctor's name and the dates with a bunch of filing cards in his briefcase. He pretty well knew what he wanted."

"You know, Mrs. Hano, I think I should take a look at that correspondence. Could you help me find it?"

She did.

The letter Doherty had wanted to see came out of a carton labeled "Box 3, W.M. Correspondence (copies)." Most of it was devoted to telling a friend at Harvard of the way in which one must go about his hobby of collecting Navajo history—of knowing the season and the place where certain stories should be told, and the social ritual of brewing the coffee, of preparing the "mountain tobacco" to be rolled in corn shucks and smoked, and of assuring each of the elders assembled in the hogan that you really wanted to know the story he had to tell. Leaphorn found himself smiling as he read it, thinking how nothing had changed from that day in 1881. The old traditionalist still, as Matthews reported it, refrained from "telling the complete story," and would hold something back, passing the account along to the next speaker, so that all of it would not emerge "from one man's mouth."

True as that material remained, it couldn't have been what had drawn Doherty here. That came on the final page. There Matthews reported that "many of these old fellows take great pleasure in misleading us whites, trying to see how gullible we will be. That, of course, makes it necessary for us *belagaana* who are serious about understanding their culture to make sure that we don't swallow stories which come just 'from one man's mouth.'

"One of their sources of private amusement is tales of how they have misled this plague of gold prospectors—the men who swarmed into these mountains with their greed inspired by the great discoveries in California and the Black Hills. For example, the records here at Wingate suggest the famous 'Lost Adams diggings,' of which I have told you previously, are 'two days travel' from the fort, and the equally notorious 'Golden Calf' bonanza was also said to be 'an easy day's ride' from our post here. Among the gold seekers, the universally accepted dogma is that the direction from here is south, over the Zuñi Mountains. My old, old friend Anson Bai tells me, and the same comes from other mouths, that both of those gold deposits were actually found in the opposite direction—north of the fort toward Mesa de los Lobos and Coyote Canyon. They say this misdirection was provided deliberately by various Navajo guides partly because of these people's ineffable sense of humor and partly out of patriotism. They understand that the worst thing that can happen to a tribe is to have whites discover gold deposits on the tribe's land."

Leaphorn reread the letter, returned it to its place, and closed the box.

"You don't need a copy?"

"No thanks," Leaphorn said. "I can remember it."

"You read that last part?"

Leaphorn nodded.

"Like what happened to those tribes in California," Mrs. Hano said. "Pretty well exterminated. The Nez Perce, and the people up in the Dakotas."

Mrs. Hano was a Zuñi married to a Hopi, Leaphorn remembered. But if he had her family properly sorted out, then one of her daughters married an Osage. Finding oil on Osage land had pretty well killed off that tribe.

"Mr. Doherty had you make copies of that letter. Is that right?"

"Just one," Mrs. Hano said. "He said he was in a hurry."

"Did he say why?"

Mrs. Hano shook her head. "None of my business, and I didn't ask. I remembered that Mr. McKay was in a hurry, too. He had someone waiting for him in his car."

"He did? Did he say who?"

"No. I noticed it was a woman, and I told him to bring her on in to be comfortable, and he said she was taking a nap and he didn't want to bother her."

"A woman? Young. Old. Indian. White. Did you recognize her?"

Mrs. Hano laughed. "Questions. Questions. I just got a glimpse. Just enough to think Mr. McKay might have had his wife with him." She gave Leaphorn a wry look. "Then when Mr. Denton killed Mr. McKay and Mr. Denton's wife went away, I got to thinking maybe it wasn't Mr. McKay's wife napping in his car."

EIGHT

BEFORE LEAPHORN LEFT the archives building, he hurried things along by getting Mrs. Hano to call the fort security number and have someone go down and unlock the gate on the road that led into the area where the TPL crews were converting rocket fuel into plastic explosives and, beyond that, into the infinity of bunkers.

The call turned out to be needless. The guard was a retired Gallup cop who recognized Leaphorn. He also was one of those who had earned a little overtime that Halloween night five years earlier helping the McKinley County sheriff's office in its fruitless hunt for what the guard called "those damned kids with their practical jokes."

And maybe the guard was right. Change the maybe to probably. What Leaphorn had learned in the archives had jarred his self-confidence. He seemed to have misjudged McKay, for starters. At least he wasn't the sort of con artist Leaphorn had presumed. And a huge doubt had clouded his certainty about Wiley Denton's missing wife. Maybe everyone was right about her except her parents, who had the good reason of loving her, plus Denton and himself. Maybe he really was a romantic, as both Emma and Louisa labeled him. Perhaps Denton could claim love, or love plus a frail ego that couldn't tolerate this betrayal, for his own self-deception. Or perhaps that same frail ego had triggered Denton into a double murder when he learned his wife had betrayed him.

Leaphorn drove past miles of bunkers, having intended to refresh his very rusty memory of the fort's layout and stimulate some new ideas. Instead he was concentrating on reassessing his old obsession with the fate of Linda Denton. If the woman in McKay's car had been Linda, if she had gone with McKay to tell Wiley she was leaving him for a new, young, and handsome lover, an enraged Denton might have shot them both. But then he could hardly expect even a very friendly local judge would slap his wrist on a self-defense plea. A double homicide including one's wife, a local girl, would have probably drawn a life term. So Denton shot both but hid Linda's body.

But no. Denton's housekeeper had been there. She'd called the police. She would have known.

Yet the newspaper ads urging Linda to come home looked exactly like a cover. Leaphorn went over it again without finding a logical way to make Wiley Denton a double murderer. Finally he drove up the slope where the southern boundary of the old fort had been expanded into the Zuñi Mountains' foothills and parked at the ruins of a small prehistoric pueblo.

He'd been there when he was a very new cop. Someone had complained that an official at the base had excavated the site, a possible violation of the federal antiquities act. It wasn't Navajo Tribal Police business, but the *Gallup Independent* had reported that Officer

Leaphorn had just been awarded a master's degree in anthropology. Thus he was sent out to take a look, had reported the site was probably a very late Anasazi outpost with no genuine evidence of looting apparent. Nothing had come of it, except Leaphorn remembered the hilltop offered a superb view of the fort below and the red rock high country across Interstate 40 and the railroad to the south. This afternoon he needed something like that to look at to restore his spirits.

He parked, sat on the tumbled wall of the ruin, and tried to fit what he'd learned from Mrs. Hano into the puzzle of Linda Denton. He found that McKay had stopped being a closed case and had become a sort of mystery himself. Denton, too, seemed to have a different role in this odd conundrum. And maybe even young Mr. Doherty. Cowboy Dashee had given the impression that Denton might be the suspect of choice in the theory of the Doherty homicide the Bureau was developing. What did the Federals know that he didn't? Probably a lot.

The sun was low now, spreading the long shadow of this hill across the empty road below, and giving a shape to the rows of huge, half-buried quonset huts spread for miles below. He looked at them awhile, watched the shadows spread, counted the bunkers in one section, tried to estimate their number, and finally guessed at a thousand, more or less. But it told him only that he had to know more about McKay and Doherty and Denton before he could solve this nagging question of what had happened to a young woman named Linda.

NINE

YESTERDAY HAD BEEN as bad for Officer
Bernadette Manuelito as it had been for Lieutenant Joe Leaphorn, retired. A lot of exercise
and frustration, capped off with a painful blow
to the self-confidence.

Bernie had spent the day trying to take a
look into every canyon, arroyo, and wash that
drained the west slope of the Chuska in the
area prescribed by the mileage limit suggested by Thomas Doherty's Zip Lube sticker.
While that territorial description included a
relatively small area of mountain slope, it involved a lot of back-and-forth and up-and-
down driving to locate drainages, and literally

miles of walking. She had accumulated pretty much the same mixture of burrs and stickers on her pant legs and socks as had the late Mr. Doherty, with the exception of the goathead seeds of the puncturevine she'd seen in the rubber soles of his shoes. Thus she concluded that the drainages she'd explored lacked the cool damp spots where Doherty had been. Or, more likely, her entire idea was half-baked nonsense.

Bernie might have dropped her one-woman campaign as useless had it not been for the call she made to the dispatcher on her way home. Rudy Nez was dispatching again. Rudy said there were no calls or messages for her. Quiet day, in fact. A couple of driving-under-the-influence arrests, a domestic violence call, and so forth. And a couple of Feds had come in with Captain Nakai from Window Rock and had a meeting with Captain Largo, and the radio on unit nine was out of service again and Elliot called in for a backup out at Red Valley and then called in and said he didn't need it. And Sergeant Yazzie, from over at Crownpoint, he—

"What did the Feds want?" Bernie asked.

"How would I know?" Rudy said, sounding a

bit miffed. Among Navajos such interruptions are not done. One listens until the speaker completes his speech. One certainly doesn't break into the middle of sentences.

"I don't know how you'd know, Rudy," Bernie said. "But I'll bet you do know."

"I could guess," Rudy said. "Apparently they found a pinch or two of placer gold dust in Doherty's truck. On the floor mat probably, or under it, or maybe in his shoes. And they want Captain Largo to get us out checking the appropriate chapter houses to see if he's been doing any placer mining."

"They didn't say where they found this gold dust?"

"Not to me, they didn't. I already said that, didn't I? Maybe they told Captain Largo. Ask him." Nez was irked by that interruption, and she got no more out of him.

But she had enough to put the pieces together. Sergeant Chee had turned her Prince Albert can and its sandy contents over to the Federal Bureau of Investigation. Which is what he should have done. Had to do, in fact. Not doing that would be concealing evidence in a federal felony case. She imagined the scene: the FBI agent asking Chee how he had come into possession of the tin. Sergeant Chee saying that Officer Manuelito had turned it in. And the agent asking when this had happened, the agent asking why Officer Manuelito had not left the can at the scene of the murder, the agent asking if said officer had taken care to preserve fingerprints, the agent asking if Officer Manuelito's training had not taught her that such prints might be crucial in bringing the perpetrator of the crime to justice. She imagined Chee standing there, red-faced, embarrassed, and angry at her for causing this. Sergeant Chee walking out of the office, wondering how the hell Officer Manuelito could have been so stupid. But, of course, he had to turn it in. He was a cop, wasn't he? What else could he do?

But now it was today, not yesterday. She had awakened angry after a restless night spent reliving a dozen variations of the scene just described—angry and determined to keep trying to prove she was just as smart as they were. She was going to find the place where this Thomas Doherty had been when he was shot, and if she couldn't, then she was going to resign and go find herself a dull, boring job as a secretary, or a salesclerk, or something a long way from Jim Chee.

Therefore, here she was glumly and hopelessly checking the botany of drainages on the east slope of the Chuska Mountains. The first little canyon had been much like the last one yesterday—the same dry-country thistles, sandburs, chamisa, thorns. The second one she tried was larger, looked more promising. She had made a map for herself, thinking that if it worked for the Legendary Lieutenant Leaphorn it might work for her, and, according to her markings on that, this one was on the very margins of the distance she had allowed. It was connected somewhere downstream with the Coyote Canyon Wash, which drained the Remanent Mesa, or was it Mesa de los Lobos? Bernie was not yet accustomed to the English or Spanish titles maps put on landmarks. Anyway, it was deeper than the last one, which improved the chances for the seep water and afternoon shade that were needed to add the variety required for the seeds and stickers Doherty's socks and pant legs had encountered.

She followed a very marginal track in her

elderly pickup until an unusually jarring dozen yards over boulders reminded her of the doubtful condition of her tires. There she pulled off to the side and walked. She'd found dampness in a place or two within the first quarter mile and some signs of truck tire tracks that didn't seem to match Doherty's tires. Not that she had looked at them when she had a chance, but Captain Largo had mentioned they were the same sort of Firestones he had on his pickup—and she had then looked very carefully at those.

Around an abrupt bend she saw a hogan. It was high enough up the slope to be safe from flash floods, built in the traditional octagonal shape of this part of Navajo Country, with its door facing properly eastward, a roof of dark-red tarpaper, and a rusty-looking chimney pipe jutting from the central smoke hole—the tarpaper and the pipe having by now become almost as traditional as the shape.

It was near noon but still chilly at this canyon bottom, and Bernie stood out in the warming sunlight while she examined the place—the stone building, a little shed, a fallen-down sheep pen, and a plank outhouse near the canyon bottom. The track she had been following seemed to end up the slope by the hogan, but no vehicle was there now. Nor was any smoke coming from the pipe, suggesting neither coffee nor anything else was brewing for lunch.

She walked up the track to the foot of the slope, went through the polite formula of shouting greetings, and waiting, and shouting again, and waiting, until the visitor was assured either that no one was at home, or, if they were, they didn't want to be bothered.

Finding the hogan was a disappointment. It seemed to make it less likely that Doherty would be finding his gold dust upstream from an occupied residence—as this one obviously would be when the occupants returned from where duty had taken them. Within a mile she found another seep—plenty of damp earth here but no puncturevines in view.

She had seen no vehicle tracks since the hogan. Now the canyon had become too narrow, too steep, and too rocky for anything on wheels, and she saw the first signs of that epic "summer of fire" that had swept through the high-country forests of the mountain West in 1999. The stems of fire-killed ponderosa pines lined the ridge above her. Ahead, the canyon was littered with the blackened trunks of fallen trees. Some places on the cliffs were splotched with the flame-retardant chemicals dropped to check the blaze. Other sections, where the fire had spread through deep accumulations of dead brush, the rock was marked with broad streaks of black. Runoff from three seasons of rain had swept the sandy bottom clean, but above the runoff level new vegetation was restoring itself in some places, and others showed only the black and gray of soot and ashes.

All this was bad news to that segment of Bernie's brain that was hunting a murder site. The segment that was amateur botanist and enthusiastic naturalist was elated. She had before her a laboratory display of how much nature can recover in three years after a disaster. For example, she could see no sign that the chamisa that flourished around the hogan had made any comeback at all in the fire zone. The thread-and-needle grass was back, and so were the snakeweed, johnsongrass, asters, and (alas) the sandburs. She hurried along upcanyon, finding more damp places, more seeps, more varieties of plants—including infant ponderosa, piñon, and juniper seedlings.

What would be the elevation here, she wondered. Probably getting close to seven thousand feet. As the altitude increased, so had the precipitation. At this level the vegetation had been heavier, the residue of dead trees and brush thicker at canyon bottom and the fire more intense.

Bernie climbed over a barrier of broken boulders into a flatter stretch of streambed. On the shaded side of the canyon she noticed a seep where the stones were still shiny with moisture. Below that she found her first puncturevine by the usual method—stepping on its goathead thorns. She sat on the rocks to extract these from her boot soles, and noticed as she did that she'd smeared her hands with the same sort of soot she'd found on them at Doherty's truck.

It was there she saw the owl. It was perched on the limb of a fire-damaged ponderosa that leaned over the canyon some fifty yards upstream. Bernie sucked in her breath and stared. No Navajo child of her generation grew up without being told that the owl was the symbol of death and disaster. Told by someone that he flew at night to do his killing, and appeared in daylight only as a warning.

Bernie had put that belief more or less behind her. Yet it was a large owl, it was looking at her, and something about this fire-blackened place had already made her uneasy. So she sat a bit, staring back at the motionless bird, and finally decided to ignore it. The next start it gave her came when she was much, much closer. She stopped again to inspect it and noticed it didn't look quite natural. It seemed to be tied to its limb. In fact, it was an artificial owl. The sort one buys to perch in fruit trees to keep birds from harvesting the cherries. Why put it there? The only reason that seemed possible to Bernie was to warn Navajos to stay away.

More evidence, Bernie thought, that this must be the canyon. This had to be it. But would Chee and Largo and the rest of them believe her? As she considered that question she noticed another oddity. The bottom sand ahead of her looked unnaturally flat and unnaturally divided into levels. She hurried upstream.

A sequence of logs had been dug into the streambed to form four little check dams—each about fifteen feet upstream and a foot or so higher than the one below. Clearly their purpose was to slow stream flow after rains, causing the current to drop more of its sand. Gravity being at work, the first stuff to sink would be the heavy gold particles. She was looking at a gold-panning sluice, and if she'd had a shovel and a bucket, she was pretty sure she could take home enough gold-rich sand to pay for the gasoline she'd used getting here. In fact, from where she stood, she could see the hole where, just a few days ago, Thomas Doherty had mined himself a little of the stuff for his Prince Albert can.

And she would do so herself—just enough in her jacket pocket to deflate any doubters, to restore her status as an equal among equals in the world of law enforcement. Officer Bernadette Manuelito, filled with that special form of joy and exuberance produced when despairing disappointment is abruptly replaced with utter success, trotted happily up the streambed, her tired legs no longer tired, and jumped over the half-buried log into the sand.

She would always wonder if that was why the shot missed her.

TEN

IT TOOK BERNIE some small fraction of a second to identify the mixture of sounds—the sharp crack of a bullet breaking the sound barrier as it zipped past her head, the sharp whack as it struck a few yards ahead, the bang of the rifle that fired it. Identification made, Bernie scrambled for cover in the rocks along the canyon wall.

She huddled there a moment, collecting her scattered wits and making an inventory of the situation. Bernie's scramble had taken her behind a great slab of fallen stone—a place that had the advantage of being unquestionably bulletproof and the disadvantage of offering no easy way out that provided good cover. She sat with her back against the stone, unsnapped the strap on her holster, removed the pistol, and looked at it. It was a standard-issue police revolver, which held six .38-caliber rounds. Bernie had qualified with a high score at the firing range, but she hadn't developed any fondness for the thing. It was heavy, bulky, and cold, and it symbolized the one side of police work that did not appeal to her. She had worked at it, imagining situations in which she shot someone (always a fiercely aggressive male) in defense of some innocent life. In these situations Bernie had managed to merely disable and disarm the aggressor, ignoring the standard police policy of not drawing your gun unless prepared to shoot it, and not shooting unless you shot to kill. Now she knew, or thought she knew, that she would shoot if this situation required it, and shoot for the middle of the man trying to kill her.

And who might that be? A man, of course. Bernie could not visualize a woman as sniper. Probably the same man who'd shot Thomas Doherty in the back—and probably for the same reason, which would be something involving this gold deposit. As Hostiin Yellow had warned her, white men will kill for gold. She thought of that warning. Hostiin Yellow had seemed unusually forceful and emphatic about it, but at the time she had passed that off as a fond uncle trying to deal with a willful niece. Now it suggested he had some well-informed reason to think the canyon she was looking for was dangerous. Right as usual. She had a wise old uncle. Too bad Hostiin Yellow didn't have a wiser niece.

Bernie could think of nothing to do now except wait and listen. Which she did, ears straining against the silence, eyes alert for any sign of motion. Normally in such a canyon there would be a variety of birds around harvesting the autumn crop of seeds and dried berries. But the fire that had swept through here had left nothing to eat but ashes. This narrowed place in the canyon must have produced an intensely hot fire, fueled by a decades-deep accumulation of dead wood. Now that Bernie had a quiet moment to think of it, she deduced what had happened here. The same endless years that had deposited post-rainfall gold dust in the sluice had been depositing dead trash to hide it. Fire had reduced the trash to ash. Runoff had swept the ash from the stream bottom. The old secret lay exposed.

The ash deposits had survived where Bernie was huddling, too high to be cleansed by runoff water, and those weeds that thrive in the wake of forest fires had made scant progress. A few yards below, moisture from a seep had kept the soil damp. There the brown and gray were replaced by splotches of green. And there, ground-clinging puncturevines had spread—their tough-as-stone little seeds impervious even to such intense heat.

Bernie arose from the ash pile on which she'd been sitting, overcame an impulse to slip out to the damp area in search of Doherty's boot tracks—clinching proof that he'd been here, if not absolute evidence he'd been shot here. That impulse was squelched immediately by the image of someone looking at her over his rifle sights. She sat again. What to do?

She could wait here. When it got dark, she could slip up canyon, climb out—(Could she climb out? Probably, but doing it in the dark would be dangerous)—and then walk out. Out to where? The climb would take her to the top, so to speak and more or less, of Mesa de los Lobos. Southward there was the Iyanbito Refinery, but getting there meant climbing down the rampart of cliffs north of the Santa Fe Railroad and Interstate 40. No way. Miles to the east was the Church Rock uranium mine, if that was still operating. Rough country over the mesa to get there, but she could do it. About then, another mood overcame Bernie. Anger.

What was she doing, just sitting here like a wimp? She was a law enforcement officer, commissioned by the Navajo Tribal Police and deputized by the San Juan County sheriff's department. Someone had shot at her. Shooting at a cop was a felony. Her duty, clearly, was to arrest this felon, take him in, and lock him up. Why hadn't she brought her cell phone along? Not that it would work in this canyon. She had just proved that she deserved better than the total lack of respect she was receiving from Jim Chee, and Captain Largo, and everybody. How much respect would she deserve if she just sat here waiting for some of those men to come and rescue her? Or rescued herself and had to admit she had run away from her duty?

Bernie got up again, took a tight grip on her

pistol, edged to the end of the slab, and looked around it. She saw nothing. Heard nothing. She studied every place she imagined a sniper might be hiding. Nothing suspicious. The man who had shot at her might be miles away by now. Probably was. Anyway, who wants to live forever? She took a deep breath, stepped away from her sheltering slab, and hurried over to the growth of puncturevine.

Preserved in the damp earth were boot prints, some crushing tendrils of the weed. True, they were a common boot print pattern, but it was also true they had left the same pattern she'd memorized from the bottom of Doherty's boot. Another happy truth: The sniper hadn't taken another shot at her.

She walked over to the sluice, and from the bottom of the hole where she presumed Doherty had made his extraction, she scooped out a handful and dumped it into her jacket pocket. That done, she started walking very cautiously down-canyon, using cover when she could and with frequent stops to look and listen. When she reached the point from which she could see the hogan, she stopped a longer time. Still no sign of a vehicle there. She saw no sign of life. She heard nothing.

Her truck was just where she'd left it. In a little while she was pulling off the dirt road onto the asphalt of Navajo Route 9. There she stopped and just sat for a while, getting over a sudden onset of shakes before she drove home.

ELEVEN

FOR THE FIRST TIME since those awful puberty
years of high school, Jim Chee found himself
trying to find the wisdom, if any, imparted by
the "separation of the sexes" part of Navajo
mythology. As in the Old Testament or the
New, the Torah, the Book of Mormon, the
teachings of Buddha or Muhammad, or any of
the other religious texts Chee had read in his
philosophy of religions course at UNM, the
complex poetry of the Navajo version of Gen-
esis mixed lessons in survival as part of teaching your relationship with your Creator and
the cosmos.

Hostiin Frank Sam Nakai, Chee's senior

maternal uncle, had tried to explain this business of sexual relationships and gender responsibilities one night long ago—the same summer night he'd taken Chee into Gallup after his high school graduation. He'd parked in the bar-and-pawnshop section of Railroad Avenue about twilight since the primary lesson of the trip was to concern the social effects of alcohol. As the evening wore on, Nakai had pointed out a dozen or so normal-seeming individuals, a mix of Navajo, Zuñi, and whites, men and women, plus a single middle-aged Hopi male—their only commonality being that Nakai had picked them as they entered one or another Railroad Avenue bar. The Hopi soon emerged and strode down the street unaffected. The stars came out, the cool evening breeze freshened, a Navajo couple emerged, angry, arguing loudly.

"Notice," said Nakai, "both talk, and talk loud, but neither hears the other. Remember what Changing Woman taught us. Once we could talk to the animals, but when we became fully humans the animals couldn't understand us anymore because now we had the words to talk to each other about the important things. But we have to learn to listen."

Even in the mood he was in now, Chee smiled, remembering that he had not a clue of the point Nakai was making. But as the evening became night, and more and more of their subjects stumbled out onto the street, Nakai made the point clear. The alcohol they had been drinking had wiped away that human intelligence—the link that had connected them with the Holy People—and now they had lost that human intelligence without the animal intelligence they had left behind.

It was while they sat watching an angry argument between a man and a woman that Nakai explained the Separation story. The people had lived beside a river in the Third World, Nakai said, with the men bringing in deer, antelope, rabbits, and turkey, and the women collecting nuts, roots, and berries for the meals. Both genders became unhappy, thinking they were doing more than their share. The women decided they could live better without the men, and the men said they didn't need the women. The women made their own camp across the river. But each gender soon discovered only unhappiness without the other, so they reunited.

Chee had provoked Nakai's story by asking

how to handle a problem with a girl at school who switched between liking him a lot and wanting nothing to do with him. Nakai's story didn't seem helpful then. And now, years later, it didn't help him decide what to do about Bernadette Manuelito. And he had to decide soon.

Specifically, he had to call Bernie and ask her if she was coming back to work. First, he'd say, Officer Manuelito, you are about to be late for work. No, first he would apologize for being such a jerk, for losing his temper, for being rude. But where would that leave him? Where would that lead? He tried to calculate that, and found himself back at the beginning—remembering all too vividly her face. Bernie's very pretty smooth and oval face had been transformed by shock, anger, then what? Sorrow, perhaps. Or pain and disappointment. He didn't like to think about it.

"Just go home and keep your mouth shut," he'd said. Sort of shouted, really. And Bernie had looked as if he'd slapped her. Sort of stunned. Staring at him as if she didn't know him. And then she'd turned and gone to her desk and started collecting her stuff. And, of course, being a damned fool, instead of follow-

ing her and apologizing, explaining that he
had lost his temper, and asking her to help
him to figure out something to do to solve the
problem, he had just taken that damned
Prince Albert tin and walked out with it. He'd
thought he'd think of something en route to
the FBI office, but all he could think of was going to see Leaphorn. Just let the Legendary
Lieutenant solve it for him.

When he called Bernadette, and he would
any minute now, he wasn't going to tell her
about handing Leaphorn the can and the
problem along with it. First, he was going to
apologize. Second, he was going to tell her all
he had been able to find out about their murder victim. And then he was going to tell her
he thought he might know where the murder
had been committed. Next, he would tell her
he was expecting her back to work, remind
her she'd been given only a couple of days off
and that her next shift started this afternoon.

He picked up the phone, punched in the
first digits of her number, stopped, put the
phone down. First, he would organize how he
wanted to report his progress on the trail of
homicide victim Doherty.

That had started with another telephone

call he'd dreaded making. He'd called Jerry Osborne, the agent in charge of handling FBI duties in the Shiprock jurisdiction, and made an appointment to meet him in Gallup. Osborne was new—replacing Special Agent Reynald, who had been transferred to New Orleans. Chee had been blamed (or credited, depending on one's point of view) for the disposal of Reynald. Reynald had made intemperate remarks in a telephone conversation with Chee, and subsequently had been left with the impression that this conversation had been recorded without Reynald's knowledge or permission. That, presuming Chee had done it, would have been illegal. Had the case against Chee been pressed, it might have cost Chee his job for what he'd done, and Reynald his job for what he'd said. But it would also have left egg on the face of the Federal Bureau of Investigation. Thus the time-tested federal "protect your butt" solution was applied. Reynald was quietly moved out of harm's way, and Chee was put on the list of those to be ignored when possible. Osborne, however, hadn't shown the hostility Chee had expected—perhaps because Chee had started with an apology.

"Since we didn't follow the proper procedures when Doherty was found, I wanted to tell you we'll give you all the help we can now," Chee had said. "You know. Sort of making up for it."

It seemed to Chee that Osborne let that statement hang there a little longer than perfect courtesy prescribed, but maybe that was because Chee had come in expecting trouble, and not just because Osborne was pondering how much he could trust him—if at all.

"Like how?" Osborne said. "What did you have in mind?"

"Like run errands. Talk to people you want talked to. See if we can find someone who saw that blue king-cab pickup enroute from the site of the killing to where we found it."

Osborne nodded. Produced an affirmative grunt.

"Maybe other ways," Chee said. "To tell the truth, I know damn near nothing about the case so far. Have you found the place Doherty was shot? Maybe we could help with that."

"Well, that would help," said Osborne. "Your officer didn't leave us much to work on around the truck."

With that mild reminder of Navajo Tribal

Police failure out of the way, Osborne gave Chee a brief and, Chee suspected, probably edited recitation of what was known so far.

Osborne was a slender young man, curly reddish hair, gray eyes, and a pale complexion sprinkled with those freckles that Chee had found strange when he moved into a dorm at the University of New Mexico and was immersed in a pale-skinned, freckled society. Osborne sat tilted a bit back in his chair with his chin down, looking up at Chee under eyebrows as red as his hair, and recounting, in carefully phrased sentences, what the Bureau wanted the Navajo Tribal Police to know about the life and death of Mr. Doherty.

Age thirty-one, divorced single male, employed by the U.S. Forest Service. Nephew of Sheriff Bart Hegarty, deceased. Flagstaff resident. Bachelor of science in geology, Arizona State U., then graduate student, also ASU. Worked summer seasons in Forest Service fire crew program, maintained checking account at Bank of America branch in Flag, no recent large deposits or withdrawals, held library cards for both ASU and Flag-city libraries, where withdrawals showed interest in mineralogy, mining, lost gold mine legends.

Reference librarian at Flag said he had asked her to help him locate microfiche files of Gallup, Farmington, and Flagstaff papers of the dates that reported the McKay homicide.

Osborne droned through more biographical details, raised his chin, and confronted Chee with a direct stare, inviting questions.

Chee shrugged.

Osborne dropped his chin again. "Slug not recovered," he continued. "Probably thirty-aught-six or thirty-thirty, rifle fired from undeterminable range, probably more than twenty yards, less than a hundred, bullet entering back between ribs four centimeters left of spinal column, exiting through sternum, causing lethal heart damage. Death almost instantaneous, and estimated twenty to thirty hours before body found. Abrasions on left side of face suggest he might have fallen against rocks." Osborne stopped again, made that hand motion suggesting end of account.

"Rocks," Chee said. "What kind?"

Osborne looked puzzled.

"Sandstone, shale, granite, schist," Chee said. "The coroner might have been able to tell from fragments in the abrasions."

Osborne shrugged. "The autopsy didn't say."

Chee grinned. "It's said the Inuits up on the Arctic Circle have nine words for snow. I guess, living in our stony world, we're that way with our rocks. I heard you're from Indiana. Not so rocky there."

"Indianapolis," Osborne said. "And you're right. You have us bested for rocks."

For the first time Osborne's expression had turned friendly and Chee found himself looking at the man as a fellow human instead of as an uncooperative competitor. Osborne had been sent down from Denver. Chee would have considered that a move in the right direction but he doubted if a young FBI agent could consider the Gallup office a promotion. In fact, he heard it was officially listed as a "hardship assignment" with a guaranteed reassignment after three years. And then, having no friends here, probably leaving his wife (if he had one) behind while he hunted housing, he'd have to be lonely. Chee felt sympathy. Osborne needed someone to talk to. He returned Osborne's smile.

"I think it'd be tough to learn a new territory," Chee said. "I'd be lost trying to work a city."

Osborne laughed. "My very first case here," he said, "involved a fatal stabbing. No billfold. No identification. But he was missing some molars so we checked all the dentists for dental charts." Osborne made a wry face. "When we finally got him identified, it turned out he'd never been to a dentist in his life. Pulled his own molars. Now how do you do that?"

"It's a different world," Chee said, deciding not to explain to Osborne how his grandmother had done it. It involved numbing the gum with a concoction made of boiled roots and berries and using a little wire noose, etc., and was too complicated to get into here. Instead he got the conversation back to Doherty.

What could Osborne tell him about how the theory of the crime was developing? What, for example, was the motive? And was it true, as the grapevine had it, that Doherty might have been trying to work a lost gold-mine scam on Wiley Denton?

Osborne considered that a moment, decided, said: "I hadn't heard that one yet."

"It seemed pretty unlikely to me," Chee said. "His uncle being the sheriff who arrested Denton, he'd know what happened to McKay."

Osborne grinned. "Nephew or not, I think anybody curious could have known anything they wanted to about that case. The sheriff's department doesn't seem too careful about its files."

"So we hear," Chee said, also grinning. "What was it this time?"

"Well, he had a bunch of stuff copied out of that McKay homicide in the car with him."

"Sensitive stuff?"

"I guess there wasn't anything very sensitive about that one," Osborne said. "My files show it was open and shut. Denton shot McKay, admitted it, claimed self-defense in a scam that turned into an attempted robbery, pleaded, and did his time." Osborne shrugged. "Closed case."

"We need more like that," Chee said. "What in the world would Doherty want to make copies of?"

"Some of the stuff from McKay's briefcase. Maps, sketches, notes on gold assays, copies of stuff from the records out at Fort Wingate." He laughed. "He even made a copy of a State Farm Insurance business card, front and back. That seemed odd, right? So we checked out the agent. A local guy, and all we found out was that McKay didn't buy a policy. And some numbers were jotted on the back."

"Telephone numbers? An address?"

"No idea. Started with a 'D' and then three or four numbers. I guess they must have meant something to McKay."

Chee nodded. "I guess there's nothing wrong with that. Not if he just made copies." He waited a moment, and added: "Be a different matter if they let him walk off with the original stuff."

"Yes, indeed," said Osborne.

"Ah, well," Chee said. "I guess the property clerk would be a family friend. And what would it matter? Closed case, after all." Chee laughed. "What did he get off with? Anything valuable?"

"Not very," Osborne said. "Unless somebody collects old Prince Albert pipe tobacco cans. You remember those?"

"Just barely," Chee said. "I never smoked a pipe. Why would he take something like that?"

"The theory is that maybe he wanted the sand in it, for the same reason McKay had it."

Osborne was grinning, enjoying this. Chee rewarded him with a quizzical look and wasted a few moments pondering.

"Like maybe McKay was pretending it was placer gold sand," Chee said. "Using it to persuade Denton he'd found the gold mine he was trying to sell him? Is that it?"

"All I know is the can had some sand in it and according to the case records, a little of what they called 'placer gold dust' mixed in," said Osborne, "and Doherty had it with him in his truck. We found it out on the ground. As you know the ambulance crew got there before the crime scene people. Things got knocked around." Osborne's expression said that was all he intended to say about this subject.

"One more thing that might help me. Could you tell anything from the stuff in his truck, on his boots, clothes? Anything that would give you a hint at where he'd been between leaving Gallup and getting shot?"

"Not much," Osborne said. He looked at his watch, frowned, and glanced at Chee. "You're going to ask me what kind of rocks he was walking on, and I can't help you about that."

He pushed back from the table. "I can tell you he walked through somebody's camp fire, or ash heap, or something. He had soot all over his shoes. And there's something I'd like to ask you about."

Chee nodded.

Osborne studied him. About to tell Chee something. Or ask him something. Then he picked up his notebook and paged through it. "Maybe those numbers will mean something to you," he said.

"Numbers?"

"On that insurance card of McKay's that Doherty copied. I remembered I copied them down. D2187. That ring any bells with you? It didn't with us, and it didn't with the insurance agent."

"The 'D' might stand for Denton, of course. Are those the last four numbers of his unlisted telephone?"

"No. We thought of that. Funny thing to copy. Made us wonder if Doherty knew something about McKay that we don't. It had to mean something or he wouldn't have made a copy. Seems funny."

It seemed funny to Chee, too, and he jotted

the numbers into his own notebook. He'd try D2187 on Leaphorn. The Legendary Lieutenant would probably recognize them as map coordinates.

With the number and the sooty shoes in mind, Chee had driven directly from Osborne's office to the pay telephone outside the Pancake House, called the U.S. Forest Service office, asked for Denny Pacheco, and told him his problem. He needed Pacheco to check his records for the past big burn season, find out which fires the late Thomas Doherty had worked, and call Chee at his office in Shiprock.

"Just drop whatever unimportant stuff I might be working on and do it, huh?" said Pacheco. "Why am I going to do something like that?"

"Because I'm your good buddy, is why," Chee said. "And we're trying to find out where this guy was when somebody shot him. It would need to be a fire within, say, fifty or sixty miles of where he was found."

"And where was that?"

Chee explained it.

"So I plow through all that paper for you, and call you at your office with it?" Pacheco asked. "And you remember this when I need a ticket fixed. Right?"

"Anything short of a felony," Chee had said, and he found Pacheco's message waiting on his answering machine when he got back to his office. Pacheco had listed three fires where Doherty's name was on the crew payroll. One was the huge Mesa Verde burn, one was a smaller fire south in the White Mountains, and one was a little nipped-in-the-bud lightning-caused blaze in the Coyote Canyon drainage. The bigger ones were too distant to interest Chee. The lightning burn was in a narrow canyon draining the north slope of Mesa de los Lobos. "This one is well within your mileage limits," Pacheco said. "Bad hot spots due to accumulation of dead timber, trash, etc., but we got to it fast with fire-suppression planes, and then it rained to dampen it down. We let the hot spots burn out the fuel trash and just sent a man in to make sure it didn't take off again. That was your Doherty."

Chee listened to that again. Probably their canyon. He'd heard that this fire, like the one that roared through the Mesa Verde National Monument area, had uncovered interesting rock art. Perhaps it had also uncovered signs of the legendary Golden Calf dig. Perhaps Doherty had seen them.

The phone buzzed. He picked it up. Officer Bernadette Manuelito calling. Take line three.

TWELVE

CHEE SUCKED IN his breath, picked up the telephone, punched button three, and said: "Bernie. I was just going to—"

"Sergeant Chee," said the strained-sounding voice in his ear, "this is Bernadette Manuelito. Are you still looking for where that man was shot?"

"Well, yes," Chee said. "But I think we have a pretty good idea now. It looks like—"

"He was shot in a canyon draining off of Mesa de los Lobos," Officer Manuelito said. "About two miles up a little drainage that runs into Coyote Canyon. There's an old placer mining sluice there—"

"Wait a minute," Chee said. "What—"

But Bernie wasn't being interrupted. "And that's the place it looks like he dug up the sand with the placer gold in it."

"Bernie," Chee said. "Slow down."

"I found what looked like his tracks there, and the same sort of seeds that were in his shoes and socks, but I didn't stake off the scene because somebody shot at me."

With that, Officer Manuelito inhaled deeply. A moment of silence ensued.

"Shot at you!" Chee said.

"I think so," Bernie said. "He missed. That's why I called in, really. I didn't see him and maybe he wasn't shooting at me, but I thought I should report it. And find out whether I'm still suspended."

"Somebody shot at you!" Chee shouted. "Are you all right? Where are you? Where are you calling from?"

"I'm home," Bernie said. "But you didn't answer me. Am I still suspended?"

"You never were suspended," Chee said. From there the conversation settled into a relatively normal pace, with Chee shutting up and letting Officer Manuelito give an uninterrupted account of her afternoon. It wasn't until it had ended and Chee was leaning back in his chair, shocked, feeling stunned, digesting the fact that Bernie Manuelito might well have been killed, that he remembered that he had forgotten to apologize.

He'd need to report all this to Captain Largo, but Largo wasn't in his office today. Chee picked up the telephone again. He'd call Osborne, tell him the probable site of the Doherty homicide had been found, tell him an officer had been shot at there, and give him the details. He'd enjoy doing that. But halfway through punching in the numbers, he hung up. Officer Bernadette Manuelito was coming in. Officer Manuelito deserved to make her own report.

THIRTEEN

THE CAR ROLLING to a stop in the parking lot of the McDonald's where Joe Leaphorn was eating a hamburger was a shiny black latest version of Jaguar's Vanden Plas sedan—which Leaphorn guessed was the only one of its vintage in Gallup. The man climbing out of it seemed totally out of character for the car. He wore rumpled jeans, a plaid work shirt, and a gimme cap decorated with a trucking company's decal. It shaded a slightly lopsided and weather-beaten face with a mouth that was too large for it.

Wiley Denton. He'd said he'd meet Leaphorn at the McDonald's at 12:15 P.M. and came through the entrance twenty-three seconds early.

Leaphorn stood and motioned Denton over to his booth. They shook hands, and sat.

"I guess I owe you an apology," Denton said.

"How's that?"

"Last time I talked to you, I mean, before calling you down at Window Rock this morning, I hung up on you. Called you a son of a bitch. I shouldn't have said that. Sorry about that."

"I've been called that several times," Leaphorn said. "Before and since."

"I remember I was pretty pissed off at the time. Didn't mean to give any offense."

"None taken," Leaphorn said.

"Hope not," said Denton, "because I'm going to ask you for a favor. I'd like to get you to do some work for me."

Leaphorn considered this a moment, looked at Denton, who was studying his reaction, and waved over at the service counter. "You want to get yourself something to eat?"

"No," Denton said. He glanced around at the lunchroom crowded with the noontime hungry. "What I'd rather do, if you've got the time, is go out to the house where we could talk with some privacy." He pushed back his chair, then stopped. "Unless you're just not interested."

Leaphorn was definitely interested. "Let's go have a talk," he said.

Denton's house and its grounds occupied an expanse of the high slope that looked down on Gallup, Interstate 40 and the railroad below, and, fifty miles to the east, the shape of Mount Taylor—the Navajo's sacred Turquoise Mountain. Leaphorn had seen a few more imposing residences, most of them in Aspen, where the moguls of Silicon Valley and the entertainment industry had been buying five-million-dollar houses and tearing them down to make room for fifty-million-dollar houses, but by Four Corners standards this place was a mansion. Denton pushed the proper button and the iron gate slid open, groaning and shrieking, to admit them to the drive. A little past the halfway point the gate stopped.

"Well, hell," Denton said, and jammed the heel of his hand down on the car horn. "I told George to fix that damn thing."

"Sounds like it needs greasing," Leaphorn said.

"I think George needs some greasing, too,"

Denton said. "He hasn't been good for much since—ah, since I went away and did my time."

A tall, narrow-faced man wearing a red nylon windbreaker was hurrying toward them. Leaphorn first noticed he was a Navajo with the western Navajo shape of broad shoulders and narrow hips, then that he had a nose which seemed to have been bent, that the face was familiar. Finally he recognized George Billie.

"You got back early, Mr. Denton," Billie said. "I was just about to take care of that gate."

"Well, get it open now," Denton said. "And then get it fixed."

"Okay," Billie said. He had glanced at Leaphorn, glanced again, and then looked quickly away.

"*Ya eeh teh,* Mr. Billie," Leaphorn said. "How is life treating you these days?"

"All right," Billie said. He put his shoulder to the gate and pushed it open. Denton drove through.

"You and George know one another," Denton said. "I bet I can guess how that happened. He said he was a wild kid. Did time for this and that before he quit drinking."

Denton pushed another button, raising one of the three garage doors. They drove in. "He's been working here for several years now. Pretty fair help, and Linda liked him. She thought he was sweet." Denton chuckled at this description as they exited the garage and entered the house. Denton ushered Leaphorn through a foyer and down a hallway into a spacious office.

"Have a seat," he said. "And how about a drink?"

Leaphorn opted for a glass of water, or coffee if available.

"Mrs. Mendoza," Denton shouted. "Gloria." He awaited a response, got none, and disappeared back down the hall. Leaphorn studied the office. Its expanse of windows looked out across a thousand square miles of green, tan, and pink, with the shade of colors changing under a sky full of those dry autumn clouds. The view was spectacular, but Leaphorn was more interested in the interior decorations. A section of wall behind Denton's desk was occupied with photographs of Mrs. Linda Denton, a blonde, blue-eyed girl smiling shyly and wearing oval glasses, who was every bit as beautiful as all he'd heard. Other photographs, some in color, some black-and-white copies of old photos, some aerials, and all in various sizes and shapes, hung on two of the walls. Denton himself appeared in only one of them, a much younger version of him standing with two other soldiers in Green Beret camouflage attire by the side door of a helicopter. In most of the photos mining was the subject, and the exceptions seemed to Leaphorn to be views of canyons, ridges, or cliffs where mining was a possibility for the future. He edged around the room, examining photographs of nineteenth-century prospectors working at sluices, smiling at the camera in assay offices, leading pack mules, or digging along dry streambeds. He recognized Arizona's Superstition Mountains in one photograph, the Navajo Nation's own Beautiful Mountain in another, and—in the largest one of all—a mural-sized blowup of part of Mesa de los Lobos. That, being east of Gallup, probably included Navajo land, Bureau of Land Management land, and private land. In other words, it would be a part of the "Checkerboard Reservation."

He was studying that when Denton reappeared, carrying a tea tray with two coffee cups, cream, sugar, and a glass of ice water, which he carefully deposited on a table.

"I imagine you've heard I'm a gold-mine nut," Denton said. "Came out in the trial, and all. I made my money in oil and natural gas leases, but gold's where the glamour's always been for me. Ever since I was a kid."

Leaphorn was sampling his coffee. He nodded.

"Always had a dream of actually finding the so-called Lost Adams dig down south of here," Denton said. "Or that Sick Swede Mine that's supposed to be somewhere in the Superstitions. Or one of the other ones. Read everything about 'em. And then I heard about the Golden Calf and I got to reading about it. And that was the one I decided I'd find."

Denton had picked up his cup and was pacing back and forth with it, still untasted. He waved his unoccupied hand at the bookshelves along much of the fourth wall. "Collected everything I could find on it, and that's a hell of a lot of stuff." He laughed. "Mostly just baloney. Just fellows rewriting somebody else's rewriting of tall tales." Denton laughed.

"One of 'em said if you say a man's a prospector, you don't have to say he's a liar." He put down the cup and sat across from Leaphorn.

"That's sort of what I suspected," Leaphorn said. "Always seemed funny that gold deposits were so easy to lose out here."

Denton didn't like the sound of that.

"They weren't exactly lost," he said, tone defensive. "With the Adams dig, the Apaches wiped out the miners. It was usually something like that. Pretty much the same with the Golden Calf, too."

"Yeah," Leaphorn said. Sooner or later Denton would get to what he'd brought him to talk about. The coffee was good and the chair comfortable, something more important to him now that his back had discovered arthritis. He had intended to drive north today to see Chee at Shiprock, but Chee could wait. After a while Denton would say something interesting and it would give him a chance to ask questions. He had several to ask.

"About fifteen years ago one of the people working on a lease up by the Utah border told me about the Golden Calf. He was part Zuñi, part white, and he said his white granddaddy used to talk about it. Claimed the grandfather had known Theodore Mott, the fellow who found the deposit and was borrowing money to build the sluices he needed to develop it. This half-Zuñi guy showed me a little bit of placer gold. It was supposed to have been sluiced out of an arroyo draining south out of the Zuñi Mountains."

Denton unbuttoned his shirt pocket and extracted a little bottle about the size of shampoo bottles found in hotel bathrooms.

"Here it is," Denton said, and handed the bottle to Leaphorn.

"I had it assayed. A little more than half an ounce, but it is flake gold all right. You'll notice some of those little grains are pinkish and some are almost black. It don't turn shiny gold until it's washed and refined." He laughed. "The son of a bitch charged me for a full ounce, and that was back when we were having that inflation and the gold price was up over six hundred dollars."

Leaphorn shook the bottle and studied it. He noticed the pink and the black, but it looked pretty much like the stuff Jim Chee had showed him from the troublesome Prince Albert tobacco tin.

"Interesting," he said. He handed Denton

the bottle and watched him button it back into his pocket.

"The price is way down now. Running below two hundred and fifty an ounce the last time I checked the market." With that said, Denton put down his cup, picked it up again, sipped, and looked across the rim at Leaphorn, waiting. But for what?

Leaphorn gestured around the room. "From the looks of all this, I wouldn't think the price has much to do with you being interested in gold mines. Am I right?"

"Exactly right," Denton said. "It ain't the money. I want to be in the books. The man who solved the mystery. Wiley Denton. The man who found the Golden Calf. I was going to have people paying attention to me." He put down the cup, threw up his hands, and laughed, dismissing the idea. But Leaphorn saw he wasn't laughing at himself. He was watching Leaphorn, waiting again for what Leaphorn would say.

Well, now, Leaphorn thought, we Navajo are good at this waiting game. The Enduring Navajo, as one of the anthropologists had labeled them. He examined the view through the window behind Denton, the sunlight on the cliffs across the interstate and the cloud formation given new shape by the slanting light. But Leaphorn's patience was overcome by his curiosity. Was Denton mentally unstable? Probably. Who wasn't, to one degree or another?

"Mr. Denton," Leaphorn said. "Are you going to tell me what it is you want me to do for you?"

Denton sighed. "I want you to find my wife."

That wasn't exactly what Leaphorn expected. But it probably wasn't exactly what Denton wanted, either. What Denton wanted, Leaphorn suspected, was to use him as a pipeline into what the FBI was doing about the Doherty homicide. He was surely smart enough to know they must be looking for a connection.

"How do you think I can do that?"

"I don't know," Denton said. "You're the cop. Or were. People tell me you're good at getting things done."

Leaphorn didn't respond to that. He sipped his coffee.

"I'll pay you whatever you ask," Denton said. "Doesn't matter. Just look for her for as long as it takes. And let me know."

The coffee was cold now. Leaphorn put the cup down.

"Is this where you shot McKay? Right here in this room?"

Denton pointed. "There by the hall door."

"Whether I'll try to find your wife will depend on how you answer some questions," Leaphorn said. "If I see any signs you're misleading me, or holding stuff back, then I'm not interested. It would be impossible. It's probably impossible anyway, unless you can tell me something useful."

Denton's expression was quizzical. "There's talk that you've already been looking for Linda," he said.

"I was once. I drew a blank."

"And there was some talk that I'd killed her," Denton said. "And hid the body. I was supposed to think she was in cahoots with McKay and I was jealous."

"That would be my first question," Leaphorn said. "Did you kill her?"

"No," Denton said. "Hell no, I didn't."

"Have you heard anything at all from her, or about her for that matter, since she left here that morning?"

"Nothing at all from Linda. Got some calls and some letters after I ran those advertisements. None of them had anything to tell. Just people trying to get some reward money."

"Calls? How? Your telephone number's not listed."

"I had another phone line put in. Put the number of that one in the advertisements. Had a technical man come to hook up an answering machine recorder on it. I've got the tapes if you think listening to any of those creepy bastards would help."

"It might. You saved the letters, too?"

"In a file."

"How did Doherty get your unlisted number?"

"Doherty? What do you mean?"

"He had it," Leaphorn said. "Had he called you?"

"He didn't get it from me, and no, he hadn't called me. I bet that's why the FBI has been asking around about me."

"That, and all the stuff about gold mining he had with him. I'd guess they think there might be a connection with the McKay homicide and his."

That didn't seem to surprise Denton. He nodded.

"Okay," Leaphorn said. "Now I want you to describe that day for me. Everything pertinent. I know you told it all to the police then, but give it to me again now that you've had some years to think about it."

Denton did as instructed. The discussion at breakfast of what to do about the ground squirrels looting Linda's bird feeders, Linda's anticipation of her luncheon meeting with girlfriends—one of whom she thought was going to announce being pregnant. Linda planning to stop at the shopping mall enroute to look at possible presents. Linda leaving, saying she'd be back about three. Denton spending the morning in his office, not getting any work done because he was excited about the information McKay was to bring him—a map showing the whereabouts of the Golden Calf and the evidence to prove it was all authentic.

At that point Leaphorn stopped him.

"Evidence? Like what?"

"He said he'd bring a pouch of placer gold, copies of old letters from Theodore Mott to his lawyer up in Denver. He said they described the site—and its location from Fort Wingate—

in great detail. And another copy of a letter from an assayer describing thirteen ounces Mott had brought in, and a copy of the assay report. And then he said he'd have some other stuff."

"Like what?"

Denton laughed. "Well, for one thing, a copy of a contract I was supposed to sign guaranteeing him fifty percent of all proceeds from the mine. And a bunch of photographs of him placering the gold he was bringing."

Leaphorn nodded.

"I was to seal the deal with delivery of fifty thousand dollars in cash, and he'd give me a partnership contract he'd signed to a claim he said he'd already filed."

"That was all agreed to before?"

"Right. On the telephone. Two days before. That was a Monday. He said he needed to collect the stuff and he'd be out here right after noon on Wednesday to close on the arrangement. And after we'd made the deal and shook hands on it, he'd drive me out and show me the place."

"But you didn't go," said Leaphorn.

"Of course not. I shot the son of a bitch and went to prison instead," Denton said. He produced a grim smile and continued his account.

McKay had called about 2:00 P.M., said he was running a little late and he'd arrive about 6:00. He'd asked if Denton had the money there, and Denton said he had five hundred one-hundred-dollar bills in a briefcase ready to be paid in return for the map and the evidence. A little after 6:00 McKay had called in from the driveway gate, Denton had pushed the opener button, and Mrs. Mendoza had answered the front door and brought McKay to the office. McKay had laid a briefcase on the table and asked to see the money. Denton had got his own case, opened it, and showed McKay the bundles of bills he had gotten at the bank. McKay dumped them out, inspected the bundles, and put them back into the case. Then he opened the padlock on his own case and took out a map and other papers.

Denton stopped, shook his head. "Bunch of damned trash," he said. "I don't know what had gotten into me to have believed that bastard. I guess it was too many years wanting so bad to find that mine I was ready to believe anything. I just felt sick when I looked at the stuff." He shook his head again. "Sick to my stomach."

Leaphorn hadn't been there when Denton had gone before the judge to plead and receive his sentence. But he'd heard about it from a half dozen friends who had. This seemed to be the same story Denton had told the court when his lawyer was urging clemency. It had the rehearsed sound Leaphorn had listened to at all too many criminal trials.

"Bad map?" Leaphorn asked.

"It was a section of one of those U.S. Geological Survey quadrangle maps. It covered a piece of the south and east side of the Zuñi Mountains. He just drew his own set of marks on that."

"You think that's not a likely place to look for gold? But isn't that about where that half-Zuñi told you the placer gold came from?"

"Same general area, I'd guess. But hell, you can find gold anywhere. Even in ocean water. It just happens that I personally know that little corner of the Zuñi Mountains. Most of the land he had marked out is BLM or Forest Service. Public land. Years ago, I did a lot of seismograph work right where that map covered, thinking I might want to lease it for oil and gas. I've been up and down every little creek and arroyo in that whole quadrant. I didn't get any seismograph results that made me want to drill, and I didn't see any of the quartzite formations you're trying to find when you're prospecting for gold."

"You didn't trip over any nuggets," Leaphorn said, and immediately wished he hadn't. It came out sounding sarcastic, and he didn't want Denton to think he wasn't taking this account seriously.

Denton hadn't noticed.

"Wrong kind of deposit for nuggets," he said. "Some big chunks were brought in and assayed from the Lost Adams dig and the Dutchman mine, too, but from what we know about the Golden Calf, the source there must have been just quartzite with a fantastically rich mix of gold veins through it. When quartz breaks up and weathers away, the gold just comes off in teeny little flakes." Denton made a dismissive gesture. "So soon as I saw McKay's map, I knew damn well it was a phony."

The memory of this disappointment stopped Denton. He drank his cold coffee. Put down the cup, gave Leaphorn a wry look.

"The rest of his so-called evidence was photocopies. Looked like he'd had some letterheads printed to make stuff look authentic, and the name right. I've been studying this stuff for years, and I know all those names. But, hell, I could have put together a better package myself. Anybody could have done it."

He looked at Leaphorn, at his hands, and at Leaphorn again, and then just sat, saying nothing, looking old, defeated, and exhausted.

"What next? You tell him no deal?"

"I told him to go to hell. Get out of my house and take his garbage with him. And he accused me of being a welcher. Said he'd given me his location of the Golden Calf and he wasn't leaving without me signing his contract and him walking off with the fifty grand. Well, we exchanged a word or two, and he pulled that pistol out of his jacket pocket and was going to shoot me. So I said to hell with it. I'd sign the paper, he should just take the money and get out. I reached in my desk drawer like I was getting my pen, and got my pistol out and shot him. I don't usually keep a gun in here, but with all that cash in the house, it seemed like a pretty good idea."

Another long pause with Denton either remembering the moment or, Leaphorn thought, perhaps deciding what else to tell and what to leave out. Denton shook his head.

"I yelled for Mrs. Mendoza to come, but she'd heard the shot and was already on her way. I checked to see if McKay was dead. She called nine one one and reported it. The ambulance came, and the sheriff's deputies. And that was pretty well it."

Denton stood, looking down at Leaphorn. "Well, what do you think? You going to give me some help?"

"We need to fill in some blanks before I decide. I want you to answer some questions."

"Like what?"

"Like where was your wife while all this was happening? She said she was coming home after lunch."

"I don't know where she was. I thought she might have stopped off to do some shopping, but usually she told me if she was doing that."

"Did she take anything with her? A big handbag, anything that would hold stuff if she was going to be gone for, ah, say, overnight?"

Denton drew in a long breath. "That was the last time I saw Linda," he said, "and I've been

over it many a time. It was a sort of chilly,
breezy day, and she had on a tweed-looking
skirt, and a jacket, and was carrying her little
purse and one of those little radio tape play-
ers. I gave it to her for her birthday. What do
they call them? They have headphones so you
can listen to music or whatever while you're
walking."

"Just carrying a regular purse?"

"That's all."

"She was driving herself?"

"Yeah. She had a little Honda. Same one
she was driving when we got married. When
they had me in jail waiting for the court hearing, I called Mrs. Mendoza or George Billie
every day to see if they'd heard from Linda,
and George said her Honda had turned up in
the parking lot at the mall. He got someone to
drive it back to the house."

"Nothing in it?"

Denton shrugged. "Just the regular stuff.
Road maps in the side pocket, sunglasses,
package of tissues, usual stuff." He made a
wry face. "I asked George about that little radio tape player. Thought he might have got off
with it, to tell the truth. A very pricey little

gadget. I saw it advertised in one of those airline shopping-mall magazines. Think it was Cutting Edge, or Sharper Edge. Something like. Very high tech. Played discs as well as tape. Linda was into discs. Loved music."

"George didn't steal it?"

"He said he didn't. Got pissed off when I asked him. Said Linda wouldn't have taken it along with her if she didn't intend to listen to it. Good point, I guess. In the car she had the car radio, but it didn't play her discs."

"It hasn't turned up anywhere?"

"I had the pawn shops checked," Denton said. "Nothing."

"You said McKay called you. Said he'd be late. You're not listed in the telephone book, and I've been told you never give anybody your telephone number."

"He'd gotten it from Linda."

That produced a long silence.

"When? That day?"

"No. No," Denton said. "When they first got acquainted down at the café. I guess you've heard how friendly she was with everybody when she was working down there." He produced a humorless laugh. "Including me. Anyway, she heard him talking about prospecting and the hunt for old gold digs, and she told him about me being interested in that. And he said he'd like to compare notes with me, and she said why didn't he call me about it."

"Is that your only number?"

"It used to be. But after I was in jail and found out she hadn't come home and started running those advertisements asking her to call, I put in the other line." Denton pointed. "It's that phone on the little desk over there."

"Was anyone with McKay when he got here?"

"Just him."

"No one came in the car with him?"

Denton stared at Leaphorn.

"I didn't see him drive up. He pushed the button at the gate, and I pushed the button in here to open it. Then Mrs. Mendoza let him in when he rang the bell."

Denton turned and yelled down the hall: "Gloria, can you bring us another round of coffee?" He faced Leaphorn again, frowning. "What are you getting at? You think he had a partner?"

"You sure he didn't?"

"Well, no. Not sure. No way to be certain. But why would he? Are you thinking Linda might have worked with him?"

"McKay had been out at Fort Wingate that afternoon. He had a woman in the car with him."

Denton looked startled. "Who? Where'd you hear that?"

"The clerk in the records office just got a glimpse of her. When she suggested McKay bring her in, he said it was his wife, and she was sleeping."

"You think it was Linda?"

"I have no idea who it was," Leaphorn said. "I'm just asking questions. Working a jigsaw puzzle with some missing pieces. Linda originally met McKay at the café? That right? He talked to her about gold-mine legends. She told him about your interests and gave him your number. So Linda sort of got the two of you together. Didn't you have any suspicions about that?"

"Never. Absolutely damned never."

"Those days after the shooting, when you were wondering what happened to her, it would have been natural to think about that when you were—"

"No sir," said Denton. "It wouldn't have been natural. Not for me, it wouldn't have been. I knew her. She loved me. Anything she would have done, it would have been because she thought it would help me."

"And that time in prison. Not a call. Not a postcard. Nothing. It's hard to believe—"

"Mr. Leaphorn," Denton said, his voice strained. He walked to the wall of windows and stood looking out. "You ever loved anybody?" he asked. "People talk about people, and you got to be sort of legendary, and so you got talked about a lot. They said you really loved your wife."

"I did."

"Well, maybe you can understand this, then. If I can figure out how to tell you."

It proved to be a long story. Denton described himself as an old bachelor, the only child of a preacher who moved too often to give a boy a chance to make friends even if he'd been good at making them. Being bashful, being homely, he'd never really had a girlfriend—at least not the kind you'd want to have much to do with. By the time he had gotten lucky in the lease-buying business, he'd written himself off as a lifelong bachelor. He said when he saw Linda waiting tables at the café where he often lunched, he was solidly set in his loner ways. But she was beautiful and kind and friendly, and she never seemed to notice he was homely, and they gradually got acquainted. It turned out she'd lived in Wyoming before her family moved to New Mexico, and one snowy day when nobody was eating lunch there, she told him about once getting snowbound at their place near Cody, and he told her about spending two days trying to keep from freezing in his stuck pickup truck out on a drilling lease.

"I don't know how the hell it ever happened," Denton said, "but we got to be really friends. She'd ask me questions and get me talking about trying to get a wildcat well drilled, and the bad guesses I'd made, and the thrill of seeing a big well come in up in the Texas Panhandle when I was flat broke. All that sort of stuff. She was going to school part-time then at the University of New Mexico branch here, and having trouble with a geology course. I helped her with that, and before long it dawned on me. Crazy as it was, I was in love with her."

Denton paused and repeated that. "Crazy

as it was. Me old enough to be her daddy, and I was in love with her. And I never got over it and I never will." He turned to look at Leaphorn. "Can you understand that?"

"Perfectly," Leaphorn said. He had never gotten over being in love with Emma—not with her being dead all these years. And he never would.

"Then I'll tell you something that's even harder to understand. It turned out it was mutual. She loved me, too. Can you believe that?"

"How did you know?"

"All sorts of little things," Denton said. He thought about it, nodded, and decided to explain.

"You might think I'm pretty easy to fool, letting this McKay thing go as far as I did. But that wasn't normal. It was because I want that Golden Calf so damn bad, and I was getting so frustrated with hunting it, I just quit thinking. But you don't make money in the mineral lease racket without being skeptical, and if you ain't to start with, you get that way damn quick. You leave your trust at home in the closet. Your basic idea is that everybody is out to skin you, and so you're always looking and listening for a sign of it. You ever gamble?"

"All Navajos gamble," Leaphorn said. "But I've never done much of it."

"Gamblers call it 'looking for tells.' Little things that another gambler might do that tip you off. Well . . ." Denton waved at their surroundings. "You can see by this I was good at reading tells. And when the money started coming in, and people could see it was, then I got to practice on another bunch. People who wanted to get to me and get some of it."

"And you thought Linda was one of those."

"Of course I did. Wouldn't you if you looked like me? So I was watching everything she said or did. And finally . . ." He stopped. Threw up his hands. "What can I tell you to make you believe it? I couldn't believe it myself, but I finally had to admit it. Crazy, but she loved me. So I asked her why. Me being way too old and ugly. And she said . . ." Denton looked away from Leaphorn, embarrassed by this. "She said it was because of what I'd done. How I'd lived. What I'd gone through. She said she thought I was a real strong man and the men she'd been around before were really just boys. Can you understand that kind of thinking?"

"Sure," Leaphorn said. "But do you want me

to believe that, after what happened with McKay, after she dropped out of sight, you didn't have your doubts?"

"Never. Not a single—" And then he stopped, closed his eyes. "Of course I did," he said. "Sitting in the jail there that night after they arrested me. And she didn't call. And hadn't come home. And my lawyer couldn't locate her. If I could have thought of a way to do it, I would have killed myself."

"How about now? How about running those ads, having me try to find her? Do you think she was working with McKay?"

Denton shrugged. "Hell, I don't know. I wore myself out trying to figure it out—month after month after month. Never did decide. After a while I just didn't give a damn. Maybe she did. Just a girl, you know. Didn't know anything about how the world works. All tied up with music and daydreams. I don't care what she did. I still love her."

Denton started to add something to that, but didn't. He stood a moment, staring at Leaphorn, waiting for a reaction. And then he said: "Does any of that make sense to you?"

"It does," Leaphorn said. "And it made sense to William Shakespeare."

"Shakespeare."

"He wrote plays a couple of hundred years ago."

"Oh, yeah. Sure."

"I had to do a paper about one of his dramas about forty years ago when I was in college. *Othello*. Young lady named Desdemona falls in love with a rough old warrior. He's trying to explain it sort of like you were, and he says . . ." Leaphorn stopped, wishing he'd never gotten into this.

But Denton was interested. "Said what?"

"Said, ah: 'She loved me for the dangers I had passed, and I loved her because she pitied them.' That's about how it went."

"Pretty well fits Linda and me, I guess," Denton said. "How's that story end?"

"It's not very happy," Leaphorn said.

FOURTEEN

OFFICER BERNADETTE MANUELITO had spent some of her not-suspended-but-out-of-favor time off sorting through her income tax records, responding to an IRS objection to her April 15 return. Perhaps that explained her negative attitude as she surveyed the swarm of tax-paid people now congregated at the Coyote Canyon Chapter House. Sergeant Chee had overheard something she muttered and had assumed his role of mentor, which didn't improve her mood either.

"It's a political law. Like physics," Chee said. "When a federal agency gets into something, the number of tax-paid people at work multiplies itself by five, the number of hours taken to get it done multiplies by ten, and the chances of a successful conclusion must be divided by three."

Bernie responded to that with an ambiguous shrug. It had been a long day—more tiring than usual for her because she was working to establish a correct attitude toward Sergeant Chee. At first that had shifted all the way from friend to potential boyfriend to arrogant boss. During the day it had modified itself to something like fairly nice boss. This improvement in Chee's rating had been helped along by how well he'd accepted his own secondary role, with her in the primary position, as source of information for Agent-in-Charge Osborne. It got another big boost when Osborne had wondered aloud how Doherty had happened upon this place, and Chee had explained that Doherty had been the post-burn clean-up man assigned here after the fire had swept through the canyon. How could Chee have learned that? Only if he zeroed in on this canyon himself. But if he had, he had said not a word about it. He'd left all the credit to her.

After she had directed Osborne and his crime scene experts to the burned area where she had been (probably) shot at, and showed him where she'd noticed what she presumed were the victim's boot prints, this area of the canyon had been made off limits by strips of yellow crime scene tape. She and Chee, their usefulness exhausted, had then been advised to go about their business elsewhere while the crime scene folks sniffed the air, read the sand, and deduced what had happened here. But by the time they'd reached the chapter house on the way out, a New Mexico state policeman had waved them down, said Agent Osborne wanted them, and directed them back to the hogan near the canyon entrance.

The hogan now was definitely occupied. Smoke, and the aroma of burning piñon, emerged from its stovepipe. The track up the slope was occupied by three vehicles—a McKinley County sheriff's car, a Ford sedan in FBI black, and an elderly Chevy pickup. Bernie recognized the grinning deputy at the hogan's plank door as a young fellow who had made a move on her last spring when they were both working the Navajo Fair, and said "Hello, George," as he waved them in.

Not all of the smoke produced by the

hogan's stove had escaped out the pipe. Three men were awaiting them in the aromatic haze: Agent Osborne, a young fellow in a jean jacket standing with him by the door, and an elderly man, his gray hair tied in the traditional bun, sitting on a bench beside the hogan's table.

"We're having a little trouble getting any information out of Mr. Peshlakai," Agent Osborne said to Chee. And having said it, he endowed Bernie Manuelito with a sort of "Oh, yes, I forgot" nod.

"What sort of information are you after?" Chee asked. He was nodding to the old man, smiling at him.

"We found the spent round that was fired at Officer Manuelito," Osborne said. "Glanced off a rock, and it's well enough preserved to get a match." He pointed toward a plastic evidence sack leaning against the wall. "He has an old Savage thirty-thirty carbine, the right caliber and so forth to match the slug we found, but the old fella doesn't seem to want to talk about it."

Chee glanced at Peshlakai, who had looked faintly amused at Osborne's description. To Mr. Peshlakai Chee nodded again, and said in

Navajo: "He doesn't know you understand English."

Peshlakai erased the beginnings of a smile, looked very somber, and said: "It is true."

"Officer Harjo, Ralph Harjo, he's my interpreter," Osborne said. "With the Bureau of Indian Affairs Law and Order office. He's Navajo."

"Good to meet you," Chee said, and switched into Navajo. "I'm born to the Slow Talking Dineh, born for the Bitter Water. People call me Jim Chee."

"Ralph Harjo," Harjo said, looking slightly abashed as they shook hands. "My father was Potawatomi, and my mother grew up over near Burnt Water. I think she said she was a member of the Standing House clan."

"Hostiin Peshlakai may have been raised way over on the west side of the reservation. The language over there is a little different," Chee said. "Lot of Paiute words mixed in, and some things are pronounced differently."

"That might be part of my problem," Harjo said. "But he's not being responsive to questions. He wants to tell me about something that happened a long time ago. I think it's about religion. We moved to Oregon when I was a kid. I don't have the vocabulary for that stuff.

"If you get down to the bottom line, all we really want here is whether he admits shooting at Officer Manuelito. And why he did it. We're going to hold off on the Doherty homicide for now. Don't want to stir the old man up on that until we get a search warrant and see what we can find in here."

"How about the rifle?" Chee asked, nodding toward the evidence sack.

"I asked him about it," Harjo said. "He said go ahead, take it. Bring it back before hunting season starts."

"Sounds like that makes it legal," Chee said. "Now, with this questioning, you're going to have to have patience."

It began, of course, with Chee telling Mr. Peshlakai who he was—not in *belagaana* terms of what he did to make money but how he fit in the Dineh social order. He named the maternal clan he was "born to" and paternal clan he was born for. He mentioned various relatives—most notably the late Frank Sam Nakai, who was a shaman of considerable note. That done, he listened to Mr. Peshlakai's listing of his own clans and kinfolks. Only then did Chee explain his position in the *bela-gaana* world and that it was his duty to learn who had fired a shot at Bernadette Manuelito. Anything Mr. Peshlakai could tell him about that would be appreciated.

This produced a silence of perhaps two minutes, while Mr. Peshlakai considered his response. Then he motioned at Chee and his other visitors and asked if they would like to be served coffee.

A good sign, Chee thought. Mr. Peshlakai had something to tell them. "Coffee would be good," he said.

Peshlakai arose, collected an assortment of cups from the shelf behind him, lined them up on the edge of the stove, put a jar of Nescafé instant coffee beside them, tested the pot of steaming water on the stovetop with a cautious finger, pushed the pot into a hotter spot, said: "Not quite hot enough," and resumed both his seat and his silence.

Osborne frowned. "What's all this about?"

"It's about tradition," Chee said. "If you're going to do any serious talking in a gentleman's home, he offers you some coffee first."

"Tell him we haven't got time to brew coffee. Tell him we just want him to answer some simple questions."

"I don't think they're going to have simple answers," Chee said.

"Well, hell," Osborne said. He started to add something angry to that, changed his mind. "I have a couple of calls to make. Come get me when he's ready to cooperate," he said, and disappeared through the doorway.

The silence stretched until Peshlakai touched the coffeepot, judged its temperature sufficient, spooned instant coffee into each cup, filled them with steaming water, passed them around, sat, and looked up at Chee.

Chee sipped his coffee, in which the flavor of the Nescafé blended nicely with the alkaline and whatever other minerals enriched Peshlakai's water. It was a taste that pleasantly recalled to Chee his hogan boyhood, and he nodded his approval to Hostiin Peshlakai.

"My grandfather," Chee said, "as you have heard, when this woman with me came to this canyon yesterday in her duty as a policewoman for the Dineh, a rifle shot was fired and the bullet almost hit her. We have come here to see what you can tell us of that. Did you hear the shot? Did you see the one who fired it?"

Peshlakai sipped his coffee, considered the questions.

Chee glanced around. Harjo was leaning against the wall, looking interested. Bernadette was sitting on the bench by the door, her eyes on him. Chee looked away.

"They say," began Peshlakai, using the traditional Navajo form separating the speaker from any personal claim to knowledge, "that when people come to another person's property, first they ask that person for his permission. This person "—Peshlakai nodded toward Bernie—"did not ask if she could be on my property."

"They say," Chee responded, "that our Mother Earth is not the property of any person. Do you say you own this canyon?"

"This is my grazing lease," Peshlakai said, looking slightly abashed. "You can look at the papers down at the chapter house. I have a right to protect it."

"Did you think Officer Manuelito was a thief who came to steal from you? Were you the one who fired the shot?"

Peshlakai considered. "What I have here," he said, gesturing around the hogan, "the woman can have all of that. It is nothing of any value. I would not shoot her to protect that."

Now Chee took charge of the silence. He guessed Peshlakai would want to expand on that, and he did.

"There are holy things that must be protected," he said.

Chee nodded. "I once thought I could be a *yataali*, and my uncle, Hostiin Frank Sam Nakai, taught me for years the way of the Talking God, and the Blessing Way. But before it was finished, Hostiin Nakai died." Chee shrugged. "So I am still a policeman, but he taught me something of the wisdom Changing Woman taught us."

Peshlakai was smiling now. "A great singer of the healing songs," he said. "I knew him. He never joined the Medicine Man Association."

"No," Chee said. Peshlakai seemed far too traditional to want to hear that Hostiin Nakai had planned to join the MMA. He was always just too busy to get to the meetings.

"Had he been here," Peshlakai said, creating the canyon outside with a gesture of his hands, "then he would have done what I try to do." Then he looked down at his hands, thinking.

Here it comes, Chee thought. He is deciding how to tell me, and it will start from the very beginning. He glanced at Bernie, who had also sensed the long, long story coming and was settling more comfortably on the bench. Harjo, newer to the ways of his people, looked at Chee, raised his eyebrows into a question.

"I understood some of it," he said. "But did he ever answer your question? Was he the shooter?"

"Not yet he hasn't," Chee said.

"My mother told me that if you keep asking a traditional Navajo the same question, the fourth time you ask it, they have to tell you the answer."

"That's the tradition," Chee said. "Sometimes—" But now Hostiin Peshlakai was ready to talk.

"They say that Changing Woman had almost finished her work here. She was all ready to follow the light toward the west and go live with the sun across the ocean. But before she did that, she went all around Dinetah. She started at the east, and on the top of the Turquoise Mountain she left her footprints, and blue flint grew everywhere around where she stepped." About here Peshlakai's voice slipped into the storyteller's cadence, recounting the travels of the great Lawgiver of the Navajo People from one of the Sacred Mountains to the next.

Officer Bernadette Manuelito had heard it all before, although some of the details varied, and she found herself more interested in the listeners' reaction than in the tale. Ralph Harjo's knowledge of religious/mythological terminology in the Navajo language had obviously fallen far short of requirements, and he had lost the thread of Peshlakai's discourse. Harjo, she noticed, had become more interested in her than in the suspect. He glanced at her, made a wry "we're in this together" face, smiled, and sent the other signals that Bernie, being a pretty young woman, often received from young men. Sergeant Chee, on the other hand, was totally and absolutely focused on Peshlakai and what he was saying.

At the moment, he was connecting Changing Woman's visits to various places with the minerals and herbs she had endowed them with—getting into territory that touched

Bernie's botanical interest. He was also moving into her home territory—specifically Mesa de los Lobos.

Peshlakai was saying that both Changing Woman and Mirage Girl had been here, and he gestured up the canyon, up the slope. And these great *yei*, these great spirits, they had left behind here, so that the Dineh could be cured, could be returned to the cosmic harmony of the Navajo way, the materials to be used in two curing ceremonies. They were the Wind Way and the Night Chant. Here our uncles (the spirit forms of the plants) had left the seeds for a long list of herbs and grasses (only some of which Bernie recognized under their Navajo name) required for the proper conclusion of one or both of those rituals.

Somewhere in this listing Agent Osborne appeared at the hogan doorway and stood looking in, still holding his cell phone. He motioned to Harjo. They talked; Harjo shrugged. Osborne came in, tapped Chee's shoulder. Peshlakai fell silent, watching him.

"What'd he say about it?" Osborne asked Chee. "Admit it? Deny it? What'd you learn?"

"Not yet," Chee said. "We're getting there.

Hostiin Peshlakai is explaining motivations. Why this canyon must be protected."

Osborne looked at his watch. "Well, hell," he said. "Tell Mr. Peshlakai that I'm in a hurry. Just ask him if he shot at Officer Manuelito here."

Chee looked thoughtful.

"Harjo," Osborne said. "Ask the man if he shot at Officer Manuelito."

"Mr. Peshlakai," Harjo said, and pointed at Bernie. "Did you shoot your rifle at this woman here?"

Peshlakai looked puzzled. He shrugged.

Bernie found herself hoping he'd say no. She hadn't been able to visualize this frail old man in the role of sniper, trying to murder her. His mention of the Night Chant had brought back a great, great memory of the last night of that ceremony. She'd been eleven, a fifth grader, and there she stood with her cousin Harold and seven other kids—the boys wearing only breechcloths and shivering in the November cold, the girls wearing their very best ceremonial dresses and all the silver they could borrow, and shivering with a mixture of awe and excitement. The Singer shaking the sacred pollen from a flask, sprin-

kling it on her shoulders, looking above her
into the stars as he sang the prayer. And then,
that great dramatic moment that signified the
entry of a child into the fullness of humanity,
the figures of Grandfather of the Monsters
and White Flint Woman appearing in the fire-
light, walking down the row inspecting them,
then removing their terrible *yei* masks to re-
veal themselves as fellow humans. White Flint
Woman had proved to be Bernie's paternal
aunt. She put her mask on Bernie's head, al-
lowing her to see through the eyeholes the
world as seen by the Holy People.

"Mr. Peshlakai," Harjo repeated, "did you—"

Chee held up his hand. "I'll handle this," he
said.

This surprised Bernie, who had been analyzing Chee's performance and giving him a
pretty good grade. Why this abrupt, and rude,
interruption?

Chee tilted his head toward Osborne. "This
officer here wants you to tell him if you tried
to kill this young woman."

Peshlakai had no trouble answering that.
He said, "No."

"I will ask you again. Did you try to kill her?"

Peshlakai shook his head. "No."

"I have no need to tell you what we are taught about the truth," Chee said. "You have taught many others. Mr. Harjo here asked you once, now I will ask you the fourth time. Did you try to kill this woman?"

Peshlakai said no again, rather loudly, and followed the answer with a very slight smile.

Chee looked at Osborne. "He denies it."

"Finally," Osborne said. "We've got that on the record, for whatever it's worth." He looked at his watch again, said thank-you-very-much to Peshlakai, and ducked out the hogan door with Harjo following.

Chee and Officer Manuelito lingered long enough to make their polite departure. At the doorway Bernie paused and looked back at Peshlakai. "I never did think you tried to kill me," she said.

The ride out of the canyon and past the chapter house was mostly silent. When they hit Navajo Route 9 and headed west toward Gallup, Bernie decided she had to know.

"What were you doing back there?"

"What do you mean?"

"I speak Navajo," Bernie said. "You never did ask him Osborne's question. If he shot at me. You changed the question around."

Chee shrugged. "Same thing."

"Like hell it was," Bernie said. "He could deny he tried to kill me. He couldn't deny he shot at me."

Chee laughed. "As our former president would tell you, it depends on how you define the word *at*."

"It's not funny," Bernie said. "And if I'm not suspended, and if I'm still an officer working on this case, I think you should tell me what you were doing in that interview."

That produced a long silence. A new red Chrysler RV roared up behind them, way over the speed limit, noticed the police car markings, and slowed abruptly. Chee waved it past.

"I have a right to know," Officer Manuelito said. "Don't you believe I do? Think about it."

"I'm thinking about it," Chee said. "And I guess you're right. I gave him a question he could deny without lying because I didn't think it mattered whether he shot at you. I'm pretty sure he must have. What mattered was *why* he shot. He must have wanted to scare you. To get you out of the canyon. Why? What's the old man hiding? What's the secret? From what he said, he's protecting a sacred place. You heard him. Up there somewhere is a source of the herbs and minerals shamans need for the Night Chant. Need for their medicine bundles."

Bernie considered all of this, remembering how frightened she had been crouching behind the sandstone out of sight of the sniper. She felt a little hurt by the lack of importance Sergeant Chee attached to her being shot at—even if it was just to frighten her. How would he have felt hiding behind that slab, waiting to be killed? But she saw his point. He thought Peshlakai had something to do with the Doherty homicide, which was why they were here. He had been establishing some "fellow shaman good old boy" bonding, being friendly. Pretty soon he'd be coming back to Peshlakai's hogan to have a heart-to-heart talk.

"Sergeant," she said, "is it your intention to freeze out Agent Osborne? Solve this one yourself?"

Chee glanced at her, not pleased by either the questions or the tone.

"Come on, Bernadette," he said. "Of course not."

Bernie waited a few moments, said: "Oh."

Hearing the skepticism in that, Chee was frowning at the windshield.

"I think Hostiin Peshlakai has some helpful information. But I don't think he's going to tell anyone about it unless he knows he can trust them. I think it will be about this damned gold-mine business, and he's not going to trust any *belagaana* if finding gold is in the picture." Chee interrupted this with a wry chuckle. "Not many Navajos, either, for that matter."

FIFTEEN

DEPUTY SHERIFF OZZIE PRICE was almost as old as Joe Leaphorn, had known him for a long, long time, and was more interested in how he was faring in retirement than in why Leaphorn wanted to inspect the McKay homicide evidence.

"As I remember, you never were much for fishing, or hunting, either," Price said, as he slid the blue plastic basket out of its shelf in the sheriff's department evidence locker. "And you don't play golf as far as I know. How do you pass your time?"

"Stuff like this, I guess," Leaphorn said. "I get interested in all sorts of things."

"Not much interesting in this McKay homicide that I can see," Price said. He put the basket on the sorting table, sat in the chair under the window, and leaned back against the wall. "As I remember, Denton got mad at a swindler and shot him and admitted it and got off on justified manslaughter, self-defense. Wasn't that it?"

"That was it," Leaphorn said. He lifted a folded pair of trousers out of the basket and put it on the table. Next came a shirt, stained and stiffened with dried blood, a belt with a heavy buckle inlaid with turquoise, a pair of expensive-looking boots, and a leather jacket. Leaphorn held it up for a closer inspection.

"Cost a lot of money, a jacket like that," Price said.

"No blood on it. No bullet hole that I can see. Front or back."

"It was hanging over the back of a chair when I got there," Price said. "He wasn't wearing it."

"He wasn't?" Leaphorn found himself remembering Denton's account of the shooting. In that, McKay had this jacket on. He'd taken his pistol out of its pocket. Leaphorn checked the pockets.

"You worked this one?"

"We were short-handed that night. Had to send a car out to Fort Wingate. Some sort of Halloween prank, it turned out to be. Anyway, I went along out to Denton's place." Price shook his head. "Wow. What a mansion."

"You still have McKay's gun?"

"Firearms go in another locker," Price said. He picked up his key ring, unlocked a small safe at the end of the room, and came back with a .38-caliber revolver, an identification tag dangling from its trigger guard. Leaphorn worked it into the jacket pocket. It went, but not easily, and produced a prominent bulge.

"That where he was carrying it?" Price asked.

"That's the way Denton tells it."

Price looked skeptical. "That's no way to treat that pretty jacket," he said. "My wife would kill me for that."

Leaphorn left underwear and socks in the basket. He added a felt hat to the stack on the tabletop and then took out a slim black briefcase, checked the side pockets and found them empty, and unzipped the center section. From that he extracted two Ziploc bags, a folded map, a stack of papers, and a tiny padlock with a tiny key in it. He held that up.

"Briefcase locked when you got there?"

"Yeah, and we couldn't find the key at first. When the crime scene crew got there, they found it in that little pocket some pants have inside the regular pants pocket. You know what I mean?"

Leaphorn nodded. One of his jeans had such a bothersome little pocket. Dimes and other small things tended to lose themselves in it. He pointed at the bags, raised his eyebrows in a question.

"The little one is stuff found in the furniture, and vacuumed up off the carpet. That kind of stuff." Price laughed. "Not that you need it when the shooter is there, and hands you the gun and says he did it. But the crime scene boys always follow their routine. Think maybe they'll get lucky, and it will be a mystery, and they can use the forensic stuff. And that bigger bag holds what was in the briefcase besides the papers."

Leaphorn set aside the map and checked the other papers—mostly what appeared to be copies of old letters, some written in an untidy scrawl and signed by Mott, some on the stationery of a San Francisco law firm. There was also an official-looking assay report, which seemed to Leaphorn's unpracticed eye to confirm a high gold content in a sand sample. He left a single-page contract form for the last. It also matched Denton's description of what McKay had brought—giving McKay a fifty-percent interest in all revenues derived from gold-mining development of "said Golden Calf property." It was signed "Marvin F. McKay" at the bottom, but the space for Denton's signature was blank.

"How's that for a deal," Price said. "He was giving Denton a map to the end of the rainbow, and Denton was supposed to promise him fifty percent of nothing."

"And fifty thousand in cash," Leaphorn said.

"Yeah," said Price, "along with a thirty-eight-caliber bullet in the chest. You think this Doherty kid was trying to play the same game?"

Leaphorn shrugged. "Why do you think that?"

"I don't know," Price said. "But he came in here chatting with some of his old friends from when his uncle was sheriff, and then he wanted to know if he could look at all this stuff. And after he was gone, I noticed an old

Prince Albert tobacco tin was missing. Thought he might be collecting souvenirs or something. But mostly he was interested in that map."

Leaphorn unfolded the map, stared at it, turned to Price.

"This map was in the briefcase when you got it? When you unlocked and opened it?"

The question puzzled Price. "Sure," he said.

"No other maps there? On the desk? Anywhere where they might have been looking at them?"

"There were maps on the walls," Price said. "Lots of them. What's the trouble?"

"I don't know," Leaphorn said. "Every once in a while I find out I'm not as smart as I thought I was."

The map unfolded on the table before him was definitely not the map Denton had told him McKay had brought. It was a copy of a U.S. Geological Survey quadrangle map, as Denton said. But this didn't depict a section of the southeastern quadrant of the Zuñi Mountains. It was far north of the Zuñis. There was a dot identified as "Standing Rock T.P." and Hosta Butte and Smith Lake—all miles northeast of Gallup, not northwest. But Leaphorn's interest focused near the map's bottom. There a ragged line represented the north slope of Mesa de los Lobos, and other such lines were identified as Hard Ground Wash and Coyote Canyon Wash. He followed that line into Mesa de los Lobos. Near its beginning was a circled X and the tiny initials "G.C."

Leaphorn made another quick check of the map, confirming what he had already known. It was a 1940 U.S.G.S. map. Except for the few marks McKay seemed to have added in red, it was identical to the bound volume of them he had in his desk—covering all the quadrants of the Four Corners of four states. He refolded the map, stacked it with the papers, and put it neatly back into the briefcase.

Then he went carefully through the pockets and cuffs of McKay's trousers, checked the pocket of the bloody shirt, the cuffs and the collar, examined the boots and the belt—finding nothing. He replaced everything in the basket, with Price watching, leaving McKay's hat. He ran his finger along the inside of the sweatband, found nothing there either, put it atop the stack.

"With a closed case like this, I was surprised when the clerk told me you still had all this stuff. I guess no relatives showed up to claim it."

"Well, usually we'd dispose of it after the legal period is over, but we had a call from a woman. Used to be what you'd call a common-law wife, I guess. She asked about how to establish a legal right to it, and I told her I wasn't sure and she should ask her lawyer."

"She didn't come in for it?"

"Didn't give us her name, either," Price said. "That was the last we heard of her. In fact, the only one who showed any interest in McKay's stuff was Doherty. He came and wanted to look through it. Said he was interested in prospecting, and he'd heard what McKay was up to. Nobody had any problem with that, him being kin of the old sheriff and everybody knowing him." He looked at his watch. "You about done with this?"

"I heard he made copies of the map and some of the other stuff," Leaphorn said.

"I let him use our machine," Price said. "Copied the map, bunch of letters, so forth, even copied a salesman's business card."

"Why'd he want that?"

"He didn't say but I remember it had something written on it. It's in here somewhere. He reached into the stack and extracted a business card. An insurance agent's name and address on one side, and on the back "D2187" was written.

"Any guesses about what that might mean?" Price asked.

Leaphorn shook his head. "Thank you, Ozzie, for your time and your patience."

"You're pretty thorough," Price said.

"I read a book by Raymond Chandler a long time ago. The crime scene crew had finished searching the hotel room, the victim, gone through everything. When the police were gone, Chandler had his detective take a look under the victim's toupee."

"Never read it," Price said.

SIXTEEN

LEAPHORN HAD BEEN trying to explain to Professor Louisa Bourbonette the confusing business of the maps.

"I might have known," said Louisa, "that if you got yourself mixed up in this it would involve maps."

For once Louisa had no other commitments, no academic duties at Northern Arizona U., and no reason not to take a ride with Leaphorn. This one was to a coffee shop in Shiprock and an appointment with Sergeant Jim Chee.

"Aside from that," Leaphorn said, "can you

think of a reason Denton would want to lie to me about it?"

"Maybe he didn't," Louisa said. "Maybe McKay had two maps in that briefcase. He showed Denton the one Denton told you about. Denton kept it. And after he shot McKay, Denton hid it away somewhere before police arrived."

They both thought about that for a moment.

"That's possible," Leaphorn said.

"But not likely," she said. "Can you think of a reason he'd bring along two maps? You might bring two maps yourself. In fact, you probably have two maps with you right now."

Leaphorn laughed. "Actually, I have three today." He extracted an American Automobile Association Indian Country map from the door pocket, and two pages copied from the U.S.G.S. quadrangle maps book from the glove compartment.

They hadn't settled the puzzle of Denton's wrong map, nor why Denton had lied about McKay's jacket, if indeed he had, or any of the several other things that had been bothering Leaphorn. But Louisa had firmly and emphatically resolved the Linda-Wiley relationship.

Yes, Wiley was in love with Linda, and vice versa. Louisa had no doubt at all.

Sergeant Chee's patrol car was parked at the café, and Chee was inside holding a corner table. He stood to greet them.

"I owe you a big favor if you ever need one," he told Leaphorn. "Osborne didn't seem to have anything to complain about."

Leaphorn nodded.

"Is this something I'm not supposed to know about?" Louisa asked.

"Just avoiding some bureaucratic red tape," Leaphorn said.

"How about you, Sergeant Chee? Are you willing to tell me?"

"A piece of evidence got misplaced," Chee said. "I wasn't sure how to deal with it, and I asked Lieutenant Leaphorn for advice. He handled it for me."

Louisa laughed. "No rules broken either, not so anyone would notice it. Right?"

"Let's just say no harm was done," Leaphorn said.

Officer Bernadette Manuelito was hurrying up to the table, looking flustered, saying she was sorry to be late. Leaphorn pulled back a chair for her, introduced her to Louisa, told her he was glad she could join them.

"Sergeant Chee asked me to come," Bernie said. "He said you were interested in the Doherty homicide."

"I think we were just talking about that," Louisa said. "Something that got Joe involved in it."

Professor Bourbonette had been around long enough, attended enough meetings with touchy faculty prima donnas, to sense instantly that she would have been better off to have restricted herself to smiles and nods.

Officer Manuelito's face expressed unnaturally intense interest. Leaphorn and Chee looked merely embarrassed.

"But I gather no harm was done," the professor added.

"I was just simplifying matters," Sergeant Chee said.

"An item that might be useful as evidence was involved," said Leaphorn, in an effort at damage control. "Jim wanted to get it back in place without involving a lot of needless paperwork."

"Oh," said Louisa. "Okay." And noticed that Officer Manuelito was leaning forward, her face flushed, and that Jim Chee was looking remarkably tense, and that it was time to change the subject.

"By the way," she said, "one of our history professors specializes in American frontier, nineteenth century, and I made the mistake of asking him if he'd heard of the Golden Calf gold legend and that touched off a standard academic fifty-minute lecture."

"Hey," said Chee, "I'd like to hear about that."

"As I understand it, the recorded facts are that a civilian quartermaster employee at Fort Wingate, a man named Theodore Mott, was sent with four soldiers to deliver some supplies to the camp where they were building Fort Defiance. The soldiers were detached to join the cavalry unit at Defiance. Mott came back alone and resigned from his job. There's paperwork for that much in the army records. The interesting part is just talk about him finding a gold deposit on his trip."

Louisa paused. Bernie leaned forward again. Chee said: "Go ahead. This is going to be the interesting part."

"The legend is that Mott came back with a sack of placer gold. Several thousand dollars worth of it, very big money those days. He's supposed to have told a tale of having to detour going to Fort Defiance to avoid a band of Navajos who looked hostile. It was early summer after a wet winter—and the snowy winter is also recorded. They did an overnight camp in a canyon carrying runoff water. Mott did some placer mining with a frying pan and liked what he saw in the sand. On the way back, alone now, he stopped again and—the way he told it—collected the sack of gold between sundown and dark and the higher he got up the canyon, the richer the sand. When he awakened the next morning, six Navajos were standing around him. He said their leader was a shaman and while none of the Navajos could speak English, he knew enough Navajo words to know the shaman was telling him this canyon was a sacred place and being there for him was taboo, and if he came back again they would kill him."

The waiter was hovering, waiting to hand them their menus and to take their drink orders. Louisa paused while the group did their duty.

Bernie leaned forward, opened her mouth, said: "I'd like to know—"

"Yes," said Chee. "What happened next? Did he leave?"

"There's a sort of vague reference in Fort Wingate military records of Mott asking a military escort for a project, and the request being denied. But apparently he got three other men to join him and they left with pack animals, telling people they were going to be prospecting down in the Zuñi Mountains. Later one of the men came back to Wingate. He left a bunch of letters Mott had written to people at the fort to be mailed, and, according to the story, he turned in a substantial amount of placer gold at the assayer's office, and bought supplies, and headed out again." She threw up her hands. "That's the end of it. No one ever saw Mott or any of his partners again."

"Sounds a little like the story about the Lost Adams diggings," Leaphorn said.

"Killed by us savages," Chee said.

Bernie said: "I'd like to hear more about that tobacco tin."

Chee said: "Ah, well . . ."

Silence ensued.

Leaphorn cleared his throat.

"It seems a tobacco tin had been taken from

the site where Mr. Doherty's body was found,"
said Leaphorn. "Later the officer in charge
discovered the sand in this can contained a bit
of placer gold and reported it. Sergeant Chee
asked me to help devise a way to get it back
where it had been and make sure the Federal Bureau of Investigation folks would find
it there." He paused, glanced nervously at
Bernie, cleared his throat. "That was accom-
plished. No harm done. No big deal."

Silence descended again on the table.

"I've always enjoyed this drive up here from
Gallup," Louisa said. "When we pass that old
volcanic throat east of the highway, Joe always tells me stories about it being a meeting
place for skinwalkers. Where they held their
initiation ceremonies."

"She's a very patient lady," Leaphorn said,
nodding to Louisa. "I think she should have
those tales memorized by now."

"I've heard a few of them myself," said
Chee, happy to join the rush away from the
tobacco-can debacle. "In fact, I may have
made up a few of my own."

The waiter appeared and delivered four
coffees, then took their food orders.

"Well, Lieutenant," said Chee, rushing in to keep the conversation away from tobacco tins and bruised feelings, "you said you're trying to find if there's a connection between the Doherty case and McKay. I can think of the placer gold link. And then Doherty having Denton's unlisted telephone number. But I think you were aware of both of those."

"I'd heard," Leaphorn said. "I guess that's what got me interested to start with. And now I should let you know where I stand. Denton asked me to do some work for him. He wants me to see if I can find out what happened to his wife. Find her, if she's findable."

Chee looked surprised. "You think that's possible? After all this time? I've heard two theories about Mrs. Denton. One is she's dead, and the other is she doesn't want to be found."

"I couldn't give him any hope. And I told him I wouldn't even try if he didn't lay everything out for me. But I've always wondered what happened to that woman."

"Has he 'laid everything out'?"

Leaphorn laughed. "Well, no. He seems to have misled me about what McKay was trying to sell him, for one thing. And he seems to have been lying a little about what was going on when he shot the man."

"Like how?"

"About the sale deal? Well—" Leaphorn reached into his inside jacket pocket and extracted a roll of paper and unrolled it on the table, exposing two maps.

"Maps," Chee said, grinning. "Why am I not the least bit surprised?"

"Well," said Leaphorn, sounding slightly defensive, "this whole business has been about maps, hasn't it?"

"Right," Chee said. "Sorry."

"McKay told Denton the location of this so-called Golden Calf dig was on this map—about here." With his fork, Leaphorn indicated a place on the southeast slope of the Zuñi Mountains.

"Denton told me he knew it couldn't possibly be there. Said he personally knows the geology of that area. Had walked all over it. So he ordered McKay out. They quarreled, McKay pulled a pistol out of his jacket pocket, picked up his briefcase and the bag of money Denton had ready to pay him, and said he was leaving with both. As this was happening Denton got his own pistol out of his desk drawer and shot McKay. That's Denton's story."

Chee nodded. "That sounds like what came out of the sentencing hearing."

"Right," Leaphorn said. "But that's not the map McKay had locked in his briefcase when the cops came to look at his body. And the part about McKay pulling the pistol out of his jacket pocket doesn't work. Big, fat revolver, little jacket pockets. And he didn't have the jacket on when Denton shot him. No holes in it, no blood, and it was hanging over the back of a chair."

Leaphorn expanded his summary with the details of his exploration of the evidence basket and his conversation with Price. During all this, Officer Manuelito was leaning forward, studying the second of Leaphorn's maps. Leaphorn caught her eye.

"I believe this is where Mr. Doherty was shot," she said. "I think this is where the gold came from that was in that Prince Albert tin."

"I think you're right," Leaphorn said. "At least about the first part. But maybe McKay had collected it there. Not Doherty."

Bernie was looking at Chee, her expression odd, but for Leaphorn unreadable.

"Do you know which deputy found it?" Bernie asked.

"Price didn't say," Leaphorn said.

Chee, who had been studying the Mesa de los Lobos map, felt an urge to get off the tobacco-tin subject fast.

"Speaking of that McKay evidence basket," Chee said, "Osborne told me that Doherty may have also taken a business card out of it with a number written on it. He asked me if that number had any meaning to me. It didn't, except maybe the 'D' referred to Denton. How about the rest of you? It was 'D2187.'"

"End of the Denton telephone number, license plate, Social Security number?" said Bernie.

No one else had a suggestion.

"Much more important," Chee said: "Officer Manuelito here"—he acknowledged Bernie with a smile—"has pretty well established that this Coyote Canyon drainage off Mesa de los Lobos is where Doherty was shot. Doherty had worked that fire in there during that bad season a couple of years ago—part of one of the BLM fire crews. The fire burned out the brush and uncovered an old mining sluice. Bernie found his tracks in there and a place where he seems to have dug some sand out of the sluice. And while she was in there, somebody shot at her."

"Shot at you?" said Leaphorn.

"Oh! Oh!" said Professor Bourbonette. "Tried to shoot you!"

Bernie, looking flustered, said: "Well, anyway, they missed."

"And," continued Chee, "the FBI got its team in there and found the slug. They're checking it against a thirty-thirty owned by Hostiin Peshlakai. An old fellow who lives near the mouth of the canyon."

"I've heard of him," Leaphorn said. "He did a Night Chant years ago for one of Emma's aunts. Is he their suspect in the Doherty killing, too?"

"Probably. Osborne's interpreter is a little weak on traditional Navajo, so they had me interview him." Chee laughed. "Osborne was in a hurry. He wanted yes or no answers, and you can guess how that went. Anyway, he finally said he didn't try to kill Bernie."

Leaphorn digested that a moment.

"Didn't try to kill her," Leaphorn said. "Did he deny he tried to scare her away?"

"I didn't ask him that," Chee said.

Leaphorn drank what was left of his coffee, looking at Chee over the cup. "What are you thinking?"

Chee shrugged. "Not much mystery there. Peshlakai says a place up the canyon is a unique source of some of the minerals and herbs *hataali* need for some ceremonies. Like the Yeibichai. He performs that one. I think he's trying to keep *belagaani* from destroying the sacred place. Bernie heard the interview. She agrees."

Chee provided some of the mythical and theological details of Peshlakai's statement, which were discussed. Bernie mentioned the artificial owl guarding the canyon from a tree. Louisa added a bit of her anthropological/sociological information about the role of owls as harbingers of death and disaster among southwestern tribes. Their orders arrived.

Over the coffee refills, Leaphorn got to the questions he'd come to ask.

"I may be getting myself in a sort of funny position," he said. "I mean, if I do some really serious digging for Denton while I'm hunting his wife, I'm going to need to know if the FBI decides he's a primary suspect in the Doherty homicide. I don't want to get in the way. Mess anything up. What do you think?"

"They don't tell me everything," Chee said. "They'd have to be interested. Doherty had Denton's telephone number with him. He'd taken that tin can out of the evidence file in the McKay case, and from what I hear, he seemed to be following McKay's tracks. Interested in the same old mine legend. But as far as I know they have absolutely nothing except some circumstantial evidence."

"Would you mind if I call you now and then and ask you if anything criminal is brewing about Denton?"

"Lieutenant," said Chee, "you didn't need to ask me that. Of course I won't mind. If I know anything, I'll tell you. Trouble is, I may not know. How about reversing it. If you learn something, you tell me."

"One more question. Do you think that Golden Calf dig, or whatever it was, is up Coyote Canyon?"

"I don't believe in these legendary mines," Chee said. "When I was a kid I used to think I'd go out someday and find the Lost Adams diggings, or maybe the Lost Dutchman's

Mine, and when I was poking around on arroyo bottoms, sometimes I'd dig in the wet sand and pretend I was looking for placer gold. But no. I grew up. Peshlakai said there's some quartzite deposits up there somewhere, probably a little gold dust washes downstream if we ever have a wet summer. One wet year, maybe enough washed down to start the legend."

"So you're not out looking for it?"

Chee laughed. "Gold causes trouble. I don't look for that."

SEVENTEEN

UNFORTUNATELY for Joe Leaphorn, Denton had spent a lot of money on his telephone tapping system. It was modern stuff, installed by a technician, and thus it had all the high-tech bells and whistles and a twenty-four-page instruction book written in the opaque language that the specialists use to exclude laymen from their science. Leaphorn had stacked the accumulated answering machine tapes in neat reverse chronological order, wasted fifteen minutes trying to get the first one to play, and finally called in Mrs. Mendoza. She showed him how to get the tape properly located in the proper slot, which buttons to push to reverse, repeat, adjust sound, and so forth.

With that, Leaphorn put on the earphones and immersed himself in the weird world of those who read the personal ads: of the lost, lonely, lovelorn, the angry, the wanna-be-helpfuls, and the predators. The first caller to speak into his ear was one of the latter.

"I read your advertisment in the *Arizona Republic*," the man said. "I think I know where your woman is. I was eating lunch at Denny's, and there was this woman at the next table. Pretty girl but looking, you know, really strung out and stressed, talking to someone on a cell phone. Crying now and then. She mentioned running away from a man named Wiley. Whoever she was talking to, she told them she wanted to go back but was afraid this Wiley wouldn't want her, and she mentioned where she was staying. A place here in Phoenix. Using another name, she said. I got that written down, that address, along with the last name she was using along with Linda. I'd just tell it to you now, but I'm tapped out for cash, and I need a little financial help for this. I'll give you this number to call me at. Call right at three any day this week."

He followed that with a number, and hung up.

Leaphorn checked the first item in the ledger Denton kept beside the telephone.

Call 1. Haley finds number of phone booth at the Phoenix Convention Center. Answered right at three on second ring. Told me he knew exactly where Linda was. Said if I would mail thousand to his P.O. box, he'll call me back, provide her address, keep eye on her until I arrive. Description not Linda. Haley says a man showed up ten minutes before I called. Waited, took call, left. Followed him to trailer park on the highway south. Haley checked Phoenix PD sources. Parolee.

Leaphorn laid aside the headphones and went looking for Wiley Denton. Instead he found Mrs. Mendoza mixing something in the kitchen. She thought Denton was "off somewhere." He'd left a few minutes ago in his car. Did Mrs. Mendoza know anything about the tape machine and Denton's call ledger? Not much, Mrs. Mendoza said, but she rinsed her hands, dried them, and followed him into the empty bedroom where the listening equipment was installed.

"He started this when he was in the prison," she explained. "He got us to take the tapes in to the prison. He had a player there, and he'd make these notes and tell George what he wanted done about them."

"Who is this Haley he mentions in the first entry?"

"Mr. Denton's lawyer made some sort of arrangement with a security company. Haley Security and Investigations. Whoever the company had checking for him, Mr. Denton calls 'em Haley."

"Must have cost him a ton of money," Leaphorn said.

"Money." She made a sound of contempt, shook her head, and skipped through the ledger, explaining Denton's dating system, code, and shorthand. Leaphorn thanked her and went back to work.

The next call was a complaint that the reward offered in the *Boston Herald* was too small and left a number to call if Denton would double it. That was followed by a woman motivated by hatred instead of avarice. She didn't know where Linda was, but she knew she would never come back. She had fled because her husband had abused her. Now she was free, happy at last.

Leaphorn skipped the last of that one and began listening to a fellow who was certain Linda had been whisked away by space aliens. He then adopted a time-saving policy of making a quick judgment of whether the caller had anything enlightening to say.

After about two hours of this he had concluded that the idea had been a mistake. All he was learning was the peculiar nature of that segment of the population that responds to personal advertisements. A very few expressed sympathy for a man who had somehow lost the woman he treasured. But most of the responses had been triggered by greed, some sort of fantasy delusion, whimsy, or malice.

Then came another sort of call. A woman's voice, sounding both nervous and sad:

"You must be Wiley Denton," the woman said, "and I wish I could help you find Linda, but I can't. I just wanted you not to think she did you wrong. I've heard that gossip—that she was in cahoots with Marvin—but she wasn't. Not at all. I know for sure. I used to talk with her down where she worked before she married you. Just a sweet young girl. I'm praying that you find her."

Leaphorn listened to that again. And again. And then he took off the headset. He would listen to more of the calls later. Maybe all of them. But now he wanted to find this sad-sounding woman.

EIGHTEEN

WILEY DENTON was home now from wherever he'd been, but Denton was not much help.

"Who?" he asked, and when Leaphorn explained, he snorted, said: "Oh, yeah. Her. I guess she was McKay's lady friend, but she didn't know anything. Or wouldn't admit it if she did."

"You found her and talked to her?"

Denton was not in a good mood. "I was still in lockup then, remember? But I got my lawyer to go out and see her. At least he billed me for it, but all she would tell him was that Marvin was a good man at heart, just liked to get his money the easy way, and he wasn't chasing after Linda."

"You still have her address?"

"It's in the file, I guess. But, hell, if this is the most interesting thing you've found so far, I'd say you're wasting your time."

But Denton provided the address and her name. It was Peggy McKay, and the address was one of a row of very small concrete block houses built in the 1920s when Gallup was a booming railroad and coal center. "Maybe she still lives there," Denton said. "But I doubt it. Her type moves around a lot."

The woman who came to the door to answer his knock was younger than Leaphorn had expected, causing him to think Denton might be right. She smiled at him, and said: "Yes. What can I do for you?"

"My name's Joe Leaphorn," Leaphorn said. "And I am trying to find Mrs. Linda Denton."

The smile went away, and suddenly she looked every bit old enough to be Marvin McKay's widow. She moved a half step back from the doorway and said: "Oh. Oh. Linda Denton. But I don't know anything to help you about that."

"I heard what you told Mr. Denton when you

called him. That was good of you to call, and
he feels the same way about it that you do.
That nothing was going on between her and
Mr. McKay. But he can't give up the idea of
somehow finding her. And he asked me to
help him, and I said I'd do what I could. Now
I'm trying to make sure I understand what
happened that day."

She held a hand up to her face. "Oh, yes. I
wish I could understand it."

"Could I ask you a few questions? Just
about that day?"

She nodded, motioned him to come in, invited him to take a seat on a dusty, overstuffed
chair by the television, asked him if he'd like a
glass of water, and then sat herself on the sofa,
hands twisting in her lap, looking at Leaphorn
and waiting.

"I'm a retired policeman," Leaphorn said. "I
guess I still sort of think like one. What I hope
I can do is get you to remember that day and
sort of re-create it for me."

Mrs. McKay looked away from Leaphorn,
examined the room. "Everything is in a mess,"
she said. "I just got home from the hospital."

Everything was indeed a mess. Every flat
surface was covered with disorderly piles. The

worn places in the carpet were more or less camouflaged by discolorations that Leaphorn diagnosed as coffee stains, ground-in crumbs, and assorted bits and pieces of this and that; and the corner beside the sofa housed a deep pile of old newspapers, magazines, sales brochures, etc. "The hospital?" Leaphorn said. "Do you have someone sick?"

"I work there," she said. "I'm a medical secretary. Keep the record files, type up reports. I was working that day. I was trying . . ." She brushed away a strand of black hair, put her hands over her face, took a deep, shuddering breath.

"Excuse me," she said.

"I'm sorry," Leaphorn said.

"No," she said, "I was just remembering. That day I was trying to get caught up on everything because we were going to have a weekend in San Diego. Marvin was planning to close on a deal he was working on with Mr. Denton, get the money Denton was paying him, and we had reservations on Amtrak for the next afternoon. We'd go swimming, visit Sea World or whatever they call it—and I think most of all I was looking forward to the train ride."

She gave Leaphorn a shy smile. "Old as I am, I'd never been on a train. You see them go by every day here in Gallup, of course, and when we got stopped at the crossing barrier to let one pass, I'd wave at the people in the observation cars and Marvin would say, 'Peggy, when I get this deal closed, we'll take an Amtrak vacation.' The evening before when he came in, he told me he thought this would be the day. He had all the items he needed, and Mr. Denton was agreeable. So I arranged to take some of my vacation time."

With that, she paused. Remembering those plans, Leaphorn guessed, organizing her thoughts. She sighed, shook her head.

"He called me about the middle of the morning, I think it was. He said he couldn't make it into town for lunch. He said he was wrapping up some loose ends. He sounded very happy. Exuberant. He said he'd just talked to Denton, and that Denton had the payment money at his house and he was going out to get it."

"Did he say where he was calling from?"

"He didn't say. But I remember he said he had to make a run out to Fort Wingate."

"Did he say what he was going to do there?"

She shook her head.

"Did he mention having anyone with him?"

"No."

"Can you remember anything else he told you in that call?"

She frowned, thinking. "Well, he said Denton had asked him a lot of questions. He wanted Marvin to tell him just about everything about where the gold deposit was located, and Marvin said no way. Not until they had sealed the deal. He said then Denton said he wanted to know just the general area. What direction it was from Fort Wingate. Things like that. Marvin said he told him it was north. And Denton said, 'North of Interstate Forty?' And Marvin said he told him it was. He said he told Denton when he came he'd give him all the details, even show him some photographs of the sluice for placer mining in the bottom of the canyon."

"Photographs," Leaphorn said. "Had you seen them?"

She nodded. "They weren't very good," she said. "Didn't show much. Just some old rotted logs half buried in the sand and a bunch of trees in the background. Marvin wasn't much of a photographer."

"Did your husband ever tell you just where this lost mine was located?" Leaphorn asked.

"I guess he did in a general way," she said. "Once when I asked him about it, he asked me if I remembered when we went to the Crownpoint rug auction and had driven down that road that runs east from Highway Six Sixty-Six to Crownpoint, and I said I remembered. And he said it's off in that high country to the right when you're about halfway there."

"Driving east on Navajo Route Nine?"

"Yeah, I think that's the road. If we had a map I could tell you for sure."

For once, Leaphorn didn't have a map. But he didn't need one.

"Did Mr. McKay have those pictures with him when he went to see Denton?"

"I think so. He put a whole bunch of things in his briefcase before he left that morning. And—" She stopped, looked down, rubbed her hand across her face. "And after I got the word about what happened, and the sheriff came to talk to me about it, I looked through his things and the pictures weren't there."

"Did he say anything else?"

"Well, he said he might be a little late." She forced a smile for Leaphorn. "Pretty ironic, isn't that? Then he said he was a little bit troubled by those questions Denton asked. Like Denton was trying to get the information he wanted without paying for it. He said just in case Denton was going to pull a fast one— something sneaky—he was arranging something himself. He said not to hold dinner for him. If he was late, we'd go out to eat."

"Did he say what he was arranging?"

She shook her head. "I think he called it 'some just-in-case, backup insurance.'"

"No details?"

"No. He said he had to run."

Leaphorn chose to let the silence linger. Navajos are conditioned to polite silences, but he had learned long ago that they put pressure on most *belagaana*. It had that effect on Peggy McKay.

"And he said he'd be seeing me in a few hours. And he loved me."

Leaphorn nodded.

"I know everybody thinks Marvin was a crook, and I guess the way the laws are written, sometimes he was. But it was just his way of making a living, and he always did it in ways that wouldn't really hurt people."

"Do you think that he was selling Mr. Denton what Denton wanted to buy?"

"You mean the location of that Golden Calf Mine—or whatever you call it?"

"Yes."

"I never much believed in those treasure stories myself," Peggy McKay said. "But, yes. Marvin had done a lot of work on this Golden Calf thing. For more than a year. I think he was selling Mr. Denton everything you could possibly get to find that place. Whatever it was. I do."

"Do you think he pulled a gun on Denton?"

"No. Denton made that up."

"The police found the gun."

"Marvin didn't have a gun. He never did have one. He didn't like them. He said anyone who did the kind of work he did was crazy to have a gun."

"You told the officers that?"

"Of course," she said. "They seemed to think that's what a wife would be expected to say. And later when the sentencing came up, I told the district attorney. He said that pistol hadn't been recorded anywhere, and they hadn't been able to trace it."

"Yeah," Leaphorn said. "That's often the case."

"It was like they took for granted I was lying. It was finished. Marvin had a criminal record. He was dead. And Mr. Denton admitted shooting him. Why worry?"

Leaphorn thought she had probably summed the situation up very well. But he just nodded. He was putting together what Peggy McKay had told him. He was thinking that the death of Marvin McKay looked an awful lot like a carefully planned and premeditated murder. And that left him two puzzles to solve. The one he had brought with him: Linda Denton was still missing with no reason why. And a new one. He couldn't think of a reason, short of insanity, why Denton would have wanted to kill Marvin McKay.

NINETEEN

"I KNOW YOU'VE never had much use for academic methods," Louisa told Leaphorn, "but for heaven's sake, doesn't it make sense, when you're trying to solve a problem, to collect all the information available?"

His inability to find a good answer to that had led Joe Leaphorn to call Jim Chee at Chee's Shiprock office. Chee was en route to a meeting at NTP headquarters in Window Rock, the secretary said, but she'd have the dispatcher contact him and ask him to call Leaphorn. That happened. Leaphorn told Chee he was developing serious doubts about Wiley Denton's role in the McKay homicide.

He asked Chee if he knew anything new that might strengthen the notion of a connection between the McKay and Doherty cases.

"Not me," Chee said. "But I think Osborne may have been putting some pieces together. And we may be about to make a mistake. Could we get together and talk?"

"What mistake?"

"The Bureau is getting a search warrant for Peshlakai's place."

"Bad idea?"

"I can't see Peshlakai killing anyone," Chee said. "But when you invest too much time in a suspect, you're inclined to get stuck with him. I'm early anyway. Okay if I stop by your place before checking in with the office?"

"I'll have the coffee on."

"Lay out a cup for Officer Manuelito, too," Chee said. "This Doherty homicide is her case." He laughed. "In my opinion, that is. We'll be there in about forty-five minutes."

"Officer Manuelito is with you?"

"Yes," Chee said, with no explanation.

For Leaphorn, with half his lifetime spent with the Navajo Tribal Police and thus battle-scarred by years of dealing with various federal law enforcement agencies, no explanation

was needed. Officer Manuelito had been chosen by the Federals as their designated scapegoat in the difficult Doherty homicide. The fact
that she had screwed up the supposed crime
site had not been erased by her discovery of
the genuine crime site. The meeting to which
Chee had been summoned probably had been
instigated by a Bureau of Indian Affairs law-
and-order bureaucrat, and would involve the
criminal investigator assigned by the BIA,
someone from the FBI, someone in the top
ranks of the Navajo Nation's justice department, and assorted others, and Chee had
brought Bernie along to defend herself and explain how she had found where the victim had
apparently actually been shot.

By the time Chee's car parked in Leaphorn's
driveway, Louisa had the kitchen's dining table
set for four. Leaphorn's old mugs had been put
back on the shelf and replaced by cups and
saucers—and each of the four places she had
set was equipped with napkin, spoon, and a
plate for cookies.

Louisa had stopped by en route to Towaoc
on the Ute Mountain Indian Reservation
where she hoped to locate an elderly Ute pur-
ported to have an account from his maternal

great-grandfather of Ute warfare with Comanche raiders in the 1840s.

"But that can wait," Louisa said. "If you don't mind, I'll hang around and find out what's going on with this mysterious murder of yours."

"It's not my murder," Leaphorn had said. But he couldn't think of a way to tell her that maybe it would be better if she went about her academic business and left homicide to the cops. Then, too, he wasn't actually a cop himself any longer.

When the real cops arrived, they didn't seem to care, either. In fact, Bernadette seemed pleased. She and Louisa had gotten along well, and Bernie was greeted with a hug. But Chee had a meeting to attend. He looked at his watch, then at Leaphorn.

"I talked to Mrs. Marvin McKay," Leaphorn said, getting right to the point, "and she said several things of interest. One. She said McKay didn't have a gun. Had never had a gun. Always said that carrying a gun was insane."

Chee nodded. Waiting. Knowing that Leaphorn knew he'd be skeptical.

"The gun the police found on the floor by

McKay's body was a thirty-eight-caliber revolver. A heavy old Colt model with a medium-length barrel. Too big to go into his pants' pockets. I put it in the pocket of McKay's jacket—an expensive leather job. I could hardly force it in. Hard to get it out. Denton told me McKay pulled the pistol out of his jacket pocket as he was preparing to leave, carrying Denton's case with the money in it, and his own case. That would be hard to do, but possible, I guess."

He glanced at Chee, found him looking more interested and less skeptical.

"So we go to item two. No holes in the jacket. No blood on it. And no jacket on McKay's body when the law arrived. It was hanging on the back of a chair. It makes it seem sort of obvious that the shooting didn't happen while McKay was leaving."

He looked at Chee again, and at Bernie. Both nodded.

"So I'm left wondering why Denton lied to me about it. Which brings us to some other things." He described what Mrs. McKay had told him about the call from her husband, about Denton questioning McKay about the whereabouts of the mine and McKay giving him only a rough description. That led Leaphorn to the peculiar question of the two maps.

"If we believe Mrs. McKay, her husband told Denton he was selling him a map of a mine site on Mesa de los Lobos. But Denton told me McKay tried to sell him a location in the southeastern end of the Zuñi Mountains. I can't think of a reason she would have to lie about it. How about Denton? Any thoughts about why he'd want to mislead me about that?" Leaphorn asked. "Any ideas about that? Or any of this?"

Chee broke the extended silence.

"If we make this McKay homicide a premeditated murder, it looks to me like it makes connecting it with Doherty a lot more plausible. Or does it?"

"It might," said Bernie, "if we could find the motive for either one of them."

"Who owns the land?" Louisa asked. She rose and walked to the coffeepot.

"Have you run into anything at all," Chee asked, "that connects Doherty and McKay in the past? Anything that would have got him looking into the McKay stuff down at the sheriff's office beyond this Golden Calf business?"

"Not that I know of," Leaphorn said. "To tell the truth I haven't been thinking much about the Doherty homicide until now. Until wondering if it might help explain this funny business with Denton and the damned maps."

Louisa was back with Leaphorn's coffeepot. She poured them each a cup. "Have any of you checked into who owns the land all this map business is about?"

"I guess it could be owned by about anybody," Leaphorn said. "It's part of Checkerboard. Partly land reserved for the Navajo tribe that could be leased out. And some of it was granted to the railroad and then sold off into various ownerships. Part of it is Bureau of Land Management property, and that's probably leased for ranching. Maybe a little of it might be U.S. Forest Service, but I doubt that."

"You know," said Bernie, "I think Professor Bourbonette is asking a good question."

"Yes," said Leaphorn. "It might tell us something."

"I'll find out," Louisa said.

Leaphorn chuckled. "Louisa used to be a

real estate operator. For a little while when she was in school," he said.

Louisa's expression suggested she did not like the tone of that. "When I was a student, and a graduate student, a teaching assistant, and an assistant professor," she said. "Doing what you do to make a halfway decent living in the academic world. I was in charge of checking titles, looking into credit, and some price estimating. So, yes, I know how to find out who owns property."

"Great," Chee said. "It wouldn't hurt to know that."

"Another question I want to bring up. See if you have any suggestions," said Leaphorn, who was eager to change the subject.

"Mrs. McKay said her husband told her he had what he called 'some just-in-case backup insurance,' in case Denton was intending to cheat him. Anyone have any ideas about that?"

They discussed that while they drank their coffee. But no one came up with anything that seemed plausible to Leaphorn.

"And finally, how about this one. How did whoever killed Doherty get home again? I doubt if old Hostiin Peshlakai could have walked all the way from the Arizona border back to his hogan. And I doubt if Wiley Denton was much of a walker. If you agree with that, who was the accomplice and how did it work?" He gazed at Chee. "If Agent Osborne is about to make Peshlakai the official suspect, how did he solve that puzzle?"

Chee laughed. "I've been wondering about that myself. If the Feds have an answer, they haven't told me."

"Hostiin Peshlakai had a cell phone," Bernie said.

"What!" said Chee. "How do you know?"

"It was in a boot box on a shelf with some of his ceremonial things," Bernie said.

Chee looked abashed, shook his head. "I noticed that box," he said. "His pollen containers, his medicine bundle, other things. But I guess I didn't really look at it."

"Well," said Leaphorn, "that might solve the riddle for Peshlakai. Maybe he walked a mile or two from the truck and then called a friend to come and pick him up." He thought about that idea. "Or something like that."

"But I wonder how many of Peshlakai's friends have telephones," Bernie said.

"If you turn it around, Denton uses his cell

phone to call George Billie, that man who works for him," Chee said.

"Or," said Leaphorn, and laughed, "maybe Denton uses it to call Peshlakai to set everything up. How about that for linking your two homicides?"

"That would work fine," said Bernie. "Then all you'd need to go with that is a motive that fits both a superrich white oil-lease magnate and a dirt-poor Navajo shaman."

TWENTY

TECHNICALLY, it was not Sergeant Chee's day off, but he had logged it as off-duty time because he didn't want someone in authority demanding that he explain what he'd done with it. He had intended to use it to eliminate any doubts he might have of Hostiin Peshlakai's innocence. His instincts as a traditional Navajo told him Peshlakai was not guilty of shooting Thomas Doherty or anyone else. However, his instincts as a policeman were at war with that. He wanted to resolve this problem, and he had thought of a way to do it. His reasoning went like this.

If Peshlakai was—as Chee was almost cer-

tain—a well-schooled and believing Navajo
medicine person, then Peshlakai would avoid
violence. But if circumstances had driven him
to it, if he had killed anyone, he would be beset by guilt, by knowledge that he had violated
the rules laid down by various Holy People.
Thus, he would seek a cure for the sickness
brought on by these broken taboos. Shamans
cannot cure themselves.

The first step, Chee decided, would be to
ask Peshlakai himself about it. He called the
FBI office in Gallup, asked for Osborne, and
asked Osborne if he'd noticed that Peshlakai
had a cell phone in his hogan. Osborne had
noticed. Had he gotten the number, checked
calls Peshlakai had been making? That was
being done. Chee asked for the number.

"You want to call him?" Osborne asked.
"About what?"

"It's a medical question," Chee said. "I want
to ask him which curing ceremonial he'd recommend for me. You know, for being involved
in this murder case."

A moment of silence followed as Osborne
digested this. "I'm still new here," he said. "Do
you have a special treatment for things like
that? As if it was a heart attack or something?"

"I think you could relate it better to psychiatric treatment. The point is that stressful happenings get a person out of harmony with his environment," Chee said, wishing he hadn't gotten into this. He cleared his throat. "For example, if you have—"

"Okay, okay," Osborne said. "I'll ask you about it later." And he gave Chee the telephone number.

Chee called it, got no answer, decided asking Peshlakai was not such a good idea anyway. He'd take a less direct approach. He called two well-regarded singers—one with the Navajo Traditional Medicine Association and the other a traditionalist who considered the NTMA too liberal/modern. Both had listed a version of the Red Ant Way, the Big Star Way, and the Upward Reaching Way as their top choices if the exposure was to violent death or to the corpse of a homicide victim. That matched what Chee had learned in his own efforts to become a singer. The next step was to find a *hataali* who still performed these sings—ceremonies that involved dealings with those *yei* who had left the Earth Surface World and returned to the existence before humanity had been fully formed.

A sequence of telephone calls to old-timers produced the names of four shamans who performed one or more of these rarely used cures. One was Peshlakai himself, who sometimes conducted the Big Star Way. Another was Frank Sam Nakai, who had been Chee's maternal uncle, who had tutored Chee as a would-be *hataali* and had recently died of cancer. One of the remaining two, Ashton Hoski seemed to Chee the man Peshlakai would have chosen. Like Peshlakai, this *hataali* was too traditional to remain in the Medicine Man Association. He knew both the Upward Reaching Way and the Big Star Way, and he lived near Nakaibito, not fifty miles west of Peshlakai's place. The remaining prospect lived far, far to the west near Rose Well on the wrong side of the Coconino Plateau. Unlikely Peshlakai would know him.

So Chee set forth for Nakaibito to find Hostiin Ashton Hoski and confirm the innocence of Hostiin James Peshlakai. He'd used up the morning on the telephone phase and skipped lunch. In the Nakaibito Trading Post he got a ham-and-cheese sandwich from the cooler, took it to the cash register, and paid.

"I'm trying to find Ashton Hoski," Chee said. "They say he is a *hataali*."

The man at the register handed Chee his change. Old Man Hoski, he explained, probably wouldn't be home today. He guessed he'd be looking after some of his sheep grazing up near the Forest Service Tho-Ni-Tsa fire lookout tower.

A good guess. The old Dodge pickup described for Chee at the trading post was pulled into the shade of a cluster of pines beside the track. No one was in it, but a thermos and what might be a lunch sack were on the seat. Chee found a comfortable and well-shaded rock and sat down to wait and to do some thinking.

On the climb up the Chuska Mountains slope into the spruce and aspen altitude, he had found himself feeling twinges of self-doubt mixed with a small measure of guilt. That had produced a sneaky hope that Hostiin Hoski wouldn't be findable and that he therefore would be spared the sort of disreputable role of testing his faith in one shaman by more or less lying to another one. He worried those notions a few minutes, found no relief in that, and turned his thoughts to more pleasant territory. Namely Bernadette Manuelito. Bernie had touched his arm yesterday as they were leaving Leaphorn's place.

"Sergeant Chee," she'd said, and stopped, and he'd stood there, hand on the handle of the car door, looking at her face and wondering what her expression meant and what she was preparing to say to him. She looked down, drew in a breath, looked up at him again.

"I want to thank you for what you did," Bernie said. "I mean about the tobacco can. You didn't need to do that for me, and I could have gotten you into real trouble."

Chee remembered feeling embarrassed, even blushing, and he'd shrugged, and said, "Well, I didn't want you to be suspended. And, anyway Lieutenant Leaphorn was the one who got the can back to the crime scene. Not me."

"I guess I should apologize, too," Bernie had said. "I took for granted that you'd just taken the can back to Agent Osborne and explained it to him. Which was exactly what it was your duty to do, but duty or not, I was sort of hurt by it. I just didn't give you enough credit. It was sweet of you to do that for me."

And while she was saying that, she was re-

warding Jim Chee with just about the
warmest, most affectionate smile he could
ever remember receiving. He'd said something dumb, probably, "Oh, well," and opened
the car door for her, and that ended that.

Except it didn't end it. Not at all. As they
were driving over to the FBI offices on
Gallup's Coal Avenue, he had been remembering the first time a woman had called him
"sweet." It had been Mary Landon, pale, blue-
eyed, with hair like golden silk. He had been
pretty sure Mary loved him while she had her
adventure as a just-out-of-college schoolteacher at Crownpoint Middle School. But not
as long as he remained a Navajo, not as the father of her Wisconsin children. Mary had been
the first, and Janet Pete the last. And that had
been way back when they were talking wedding plans and before he had finally, finally,
reluctantly faced the fact that Janet saw him
as he would be when she had remade him into
a match of herself—another of the beautiful
people Maryland/Virginia beltway elite. Janet
had seen him as a rough diamond she'd found
in the West who would become a gem in her
urbane, Ivy League East after a little polish-
ing.

And now Bernadette Manuelito had said what seemed to have become for Chee the magic word. He thought about her. The landscape spread below the Tho-Ni-Tsa fire lookout on this cool late summer day almost extended forever. The vivid greens of high-country aspen, fir, and spruce turned into the darker shades of lower elevations where juniper and piñon dominated. That quickly faded into the pale-tan immensity of the grazing country. Shadows formed along the serrated cliffs of Chaco Mesa, and to the south the blue shape of the San Mateo rose, capped by the spire of Tsoodzil, the sacred Turquoise Mountain guarding the south boundary of Dine' Bike'yah.

"Our heartland," Bernie had called it. "Our Holy Land. Our Dine'tah." He'd always remembered that.

That had been another summer day like this, with squadrons of cumulus clouds drifting across the sky and dragging their shadows across the valley. Bernie was brand new in the NPD, and he was taking her around—showing her where a Toadlena bootlegger lived, the locale of a family suspected of stealing cattle, and some of the places where terrain caused communication blind spots, and the good places where even their old radios would reach Shiprock or Window Rock. He'd stopped beside the dirt road up Chuska Peak to check in. Bernie had got out to collect another of those seedpods that attracted her. He'd joined her, stretching his legs and his cramped back muscles, thinking that he wasn't quite as young as he had been, thinking Janet Pete had court duty in Farmington that day and they had a dinner date that night. And then finding himself comparing Bernie's delight with a landscape that offered nothing but beauty and poverty with how Janet would have reacted.

Thinking about it now, he realized that might have been the moment when he first wondered if the bright young lawyer's beauty and style would be enough to let them bridge the cultural chasm between them.

He was pondering that when he heard the tinkle of sheep bells, and the flock began flowing past the spruce thicket above him. A slender, gray-haired man and a shepherd dog emerged a moment later. The man walked toward Chee while the dog raced past the flock, directing it toward a down-slope meadow.

Chee stood, identified himself by clan and kinfolk, and waited while the gray-haired man identified himself as Ashton Hoski.

"They say that you are a *hataali* and can conduct the Upward Reaching Way, and also the Big Star Way," Chee said.

"That is true," Hostiin Hoski said, and he laughed. "Years pass and there is never a need for either one. I start thinking that the Dineh have learned not to be violent. That I can forget those sings. But now I get patients again. Do you need to have the ceremony done for someone? For yourself?"

"It might be necessary," Chee said. "Do you already have a patient you are preparing for?"

Hoski nodded. "Yes," he said. "Probably in October. As soon as the thunder sleeps."

Chee felt a sick premonition. He hesitated.

"I know who you are," Hoski said. "You are a policeman. I have seen you on the TV news. At the court trial of that man who killed his brother-in-law, and then last week at that head-on collision out on Highway Six Sixty-Six. I'll bet you have the same ghost sickness—the very same ghost—as the man I will be singing for."

"Yes," Chee said. "It is a job that causes you to be around too much death."

"Were you around the corpse of this man who was shot up in the Coyote Canyon country? That would make it very easy. That was the same man."

Chee swallowed. He didn't want to ask this question. He was almost certain he didn't want to know the answer. Or what to do with it if it was what he expected.

"Who is your other patient?" Chee asked.

"I think you might know of him," Hoski said. "Hostiin James Peshlakai."

TWENTY-ONE

SERGEANT JIM CHEE usually enjoyed driving, but the journey from Hostiin Hoski's high-country sheep meadow to Gallup's Gold Avenue offices of the Federal Bureau of Investigation had been totally glum. He had made Osborne very aware of his opinion that Hostiin James Peshlakai was not a promising suspect in the Doherty homicide. Now his sense of duty, or honor, or whatever he could call it, required him to reverse that. Not that he thought Osborne had lent much weight to his opinion or, for that matter, would lend any weight at all to Peshlakai's arranging a Big Star Way for himself. However, Chee was an officer of the law. Duty required it. Why hadn't he been smart enough to leave well enough alone?

He could deal with that, of course. He'd simply tell Osborne what he had found, try to explain the implications, try not to notice that Osborne's interest, if he showed any at all, was simply polite, and then forget it—just as Osborne would.

But another problem that had surfaced on this trip wouldn't go away. He was finally facing the fact that he was falling in love with Officer Bernadette Manuelito.

That, too, was a matter of honor. He was Bernie's supervisor, and that, under Chee's ethical code, made her off limits and out of bounds. Besides he didn't know whether Bernie shared his feelings. She liked him, or at least pretended to as employees sometimes do. She had referred to him as "sweet" with a tone and a look that was obviously sincere even by Chee's uncertain judgment. But what he had done for her had been a bit risky, even after Leaphorn's assistance took most of the risk away. Therefore, it was only natural that a well-raised woman would express her thanks. So how could he find out where he stood? By romancing her, or trying to. But how could he do that as long as he was the fellow ordering her around every day? He couldn't think of a good way. And what would happen if he did?

Chee parked just down the street from the FBI offices, pushed the buzzer, identified himself, and was clicked in. He made his way through the metal detector and past the row of cubicles where agents did their paperwork, then found Osborne awaiting him in a hearing room. They exchanged the usual greetings.

"Well," said Osborne, "what's new?"

"I've had to change my thinking about James Peshlakai," Chee said. "I think you'll want to take a close look at him."

"Why? Something happen?"

"Remember what I started telling you about a curing ceremony that traditionals have after being involved with death, or corpses, or violence? Well, I checked on that. Peshlakai has arranged one."

Osborne was sitting behind his desk, studying Chee. He nodded.

"He contacted a singer and arranged it the same day Doherty's body was found. In the morning."

Osborne's expression was inscrutable. "Was it something called a Big Star Way?" he asked. "Is that it?"

Short silence while Chee digested this. "Well, yes," he said. "That's the one."

"He told us he had to be out of jail in October to have that done."

"Out? You picked him up?"

"We got a warrant. Searched his place and his truck. The truck seems to be clean, so far anyway, but there was dried blood on a shirt. He'd tried to wash it, but getting blood out isn't easy. Blood on a pair of pants, too. It's not Peshlakai's blood type, but it matches Doherty's. The forensic people are doing DNA checks now."

Chee had taken a chair across from Osborne. He got up now, hesitated. Sat down again. He felt like a fool. And yet something still seemed wrong about this. One thing, specifically: No one is more conditioned against violence than those who spend years and years learning the curing ways of the Dineh.

"I guess he's held in the county jail?" Chee said. "I'd like to talk to him."

"Why not," Osborne said. "I hope you have better luck than we did."

"Did he say he wanted a lawyer?"

"We told him the court would appoint him a public defender. All he said was something like it being a bad business. It wasn't good to talk about."

"That's it?"

"Pretty much. Except we've found another slug in the sand out at that old placer site. It's the right caliber to match Peshlakai's rifle, but we don't have a report from the laboratory yet. And then he told us he had to be released in time for the sing, or whatever you call it."

"The slug could have been shot at anything," Chee said.

"Obviously," Osborne said. "They're looking for traces of blood, or bone, or fabric on it."

"Have you learned anything about the cell phone?"

Osborne considered that a moment. He opened his desk drawer, extracted a pencil, tapped it on the desk, and said: "Cell phone? Like what?"

"Like I was surprised he had one. Do you know where he got it? Or why?"

"The why looks obvious to me," Osborne said. "No telephone lines in there."

"I meant, who would he be calling? Who would he know who'd have a telephone number? That sort of thing. I presume you checked his calling log."

Osborne tapped with the pencil again, looking thoughtful.

Chee grinned. "Let me guess what you're thinking. You're remembering that when you checked in here, you were warned that one of your predecessors got in trouble for saying some things that maybe he shouldn't have said to me, and it was generally believed I had unethically and illegally taped that call—or at the very least had caused people to believe I had taped it. Therefore, you're being careful. I don't blame you. Part of that is true, or partly true. But we have a different situation here. We're on the same side of this one, in the first place. Besides, I don't have any way to tape this."

Osborne was grinning, too.

"Since you're not wired, I'll admit I heard about that business, and I also heard it turned out you were right. We had the wrong guy in that one. But this time it looks like we have the right one. And if we don't, if the DNA turns out wrong or we don't find other evidence, then he's free as a bird."

He reopened the drawer, put the pencil away. "So what are you asking me?"

"Who Peshlakai was calling on that cell phone."

"Not much of anybody," Osborne said. "He had it a couple of years and only thirty-seven calls were logged in that time. Most of them to his daughter over at Keams Canyon. A couple of other kinfolks, a doctor in Gallup."

"How about any calls to Wiley Denton?"

Osborne looked thoughtful. "Denton?" he said. "Now, why would Mr. Peshlakai be calling Mr. Denton?"

"How about like you'd call a taxi," Chee said, swallowing a twinge of resentment at this game playing. "Perhaps he wanted a ride home."

"From where?"

"How about from where he'd parked Mr. Doherty's body in Mr. Doherty's pickup truck?"

Osborne laughed. "I guess that would play," he said. "Why do all cops think so much alike?"

"Why don't you just tell me?"

"I don't know," Osborne said. "Yes, Peshlakai called Mr. Denton a total of thirteen times. Two of them were the first calls charged to the telephone and calls twelve and thirteen were recorded the day Doherty was killed."

Chee considered this, remembering the conversation with Bernie, Leaphorn, and Professor Bourbonette at Leaphorn's home. He shook his head. As Bernie had said, now all they needed was a motive that fit a traditionalist shaman and a wealthy white man with a missing wife and an obsession with finding a legendary gold mine.

They knew Chee at the McKinley County Detention Center, of course, but that didn't help. The bureaucratic machinery had worked faster than usual. Someone named Eleanor Knoblock seemed to have been assigned as Hostiin Peshlakai's public defender, and Ms. Knoblock had signed an order providing that no one be allowed to interview her client without arranging it with her and speaking to Peshlakai in her presence. Chee jotted down her telephone number, but he decided to let things rest for the day. He'd already made his full quota of mistakes and had enough problems to worry about.

TWENTY-TWO

WHEN HIS TELEPHONE RANG, Joe Leaphorn usually dropped whatever he was doing and hurried over to answer it—a habit he suspected was probably common with lonely widowers whose only conversation tends to be talking back to the television set. Having Professor Louisa Bourbonette adopt his guest room as her base of operations for her oral history research had taken some of the edge off that problem, and this morning he wanted to think instead of talk. The solution to the riddle of Linda Denton and the odd and illogical business with Wiley Denton's affairs with gold-mine maps hung just at the edge of his vision—almost in sight, but always dancing away.

The phone rang again, and again. It occurred to Leaphorn that Louisa had taken her tape recorder up to Mexican Hat yesterday to capture the recollections of an elderly Mormon rancher. She'd returned long after he'd retired for the night, and this damned telephone was certain to awaken her. He picked it up, said a grumpy-sounding "Hello."

"It's Jim Chee, Lieutenant. Do you have time to listen to a report?"

"It's Mr. Leaphorn now, Jim," Leaphorn said. "Or just Joe." He'd told Chee that a hundred times, but it didn't seem to stick. "But go ahead."

"I guess the bottom line is they've arrested Hostiin Peshlakai in the Doherty homicide. Found blood on his clothing that matched Doherty's type, and they're checking for a DNA match. They also found another slug at the placer site that matches his caliber. Checking that for everything, too."

"Be damned," Leaphorn said. "What does Peshlakai say?"

"He says he doesn't want to talk about it. Didn't ask for a lawyer, but they assigned him a public defender named Knoblock. A woman. Do you know her?"

"I've met her," Leaphorn said. "Long time ago. She's tough."

"I couldn't get in to talk to Peshlakai," Chee said.

Leaphorn chuckled. "That doesn't surprise me. What do you think he'd tell you?"

"Probably not much. Also, the morning Doherty's body was found—I think before Bernie found it—Peshlakai contacted a singer and arranged to have a Big Star Way done for him."

"Well, now," Leaphorn said. "That sounds a little like a confession, doesn't it?" He chuckled. "But can you imagine the U.S. district attorney trying to understand that, and then trying to explain it to a jury in Albuquerque?"

"Not a confession, more like an implication. Now I'm getting to the part of this that will interest you. Remember that cell phone Bernie noticed in his hogan? Well, he called Wiley Denton on it twice the day Doherty was shot."

That surprised Leaphorn. He said, "Well, now."

"Two calls. The first one was eleven minutes long. The second one, less than three minutes."

Leaphorn sighed and waited. There would be more.

"Another interesting thing. He'd had the phone a couple of years. Made only thirty-seven calls. The first two he made after he got the phone were also to Wiley Denton."

"Sounds like Wiley might have bought it for him, you think?"

"Yeah," Chee said. "But why?"

"I'll hand that one back to you, Jim. You met the man. Talked to him at his hogan. You think he could be on Denton's payroll for some reason or other?"

"Maybe," Chee said. "But, no, I don't think so. How about you? Do you think the two of them are involved in some sort of weird conspiracy?"

"Denton using the old man as a watchman? Maybe I've got to think about this."

"Well," said Chee, "if you have any constructive ideas, I hope you'll tell me about them. I'm going to make another effort to talk to Peshlakai."

"Good idea," Leaphorn said. "I think I'll go have another visit with Wiley Denton."

But Denton's housekeeper said Mr. Denton was not home, and, no, he probably wouldn't be back very soon because he had gone over to the Jicarilla Reservation to look at one of the pump jacks he had on a well over there.

Leaphorn left a message asking Denton to call, that he needed to talk to him. Then he got out his notebook and the map he'd been sketching out of this complicated affair and went over the way his thinking had developed. At the end of the notes he'd jotted after his talk with the Garcias, he found "Deputy Lorenzo Perez. Maybe he took wailing seriously. Is he the Perez I know?"

The woman who answered the telephone at the sheriff's office said Deputy Perez had retired a couple of years before. But, yes, Ozzie Price was in.

"You again, Joe?" Ozzie said. "What now?"

"I'm looking for Lorenzo Perez," Leaphorn said. "Didn't he used to be undersheriff?"

"That's him," Ozzie said. "But that was under a different sheriff, and that was before his wife left him and he got into heavy drinking."

"He's still in Gallup?"

"Oh, yeah," Ozzie said. "You want to talk to him?"

Leaphorn said he did, and waited. In a long minute, Ozzie provided three numbers. One was a street address, one was Perez's phone number there, and the third was the number of the Old 66 Tavern. "Try that last one most evenings," Ozzie said.

"Was he sent out on that Halloween call to Fort Wingate? The one we were talking about the other day?"

"He was," Ozzie said. "And he got all wrapped up in it. I think that was when he was having wife troubles, and maybe it gave him something else to think about. Anyway, he kept nagging at the sheriff to look into it more. He thought Denton had killed his wife out there. Kept thinking it even after it was so damned obvious Denton couldn't have done it." Ozzie laughed. "Denton was busy at home killing McKay."

Now Leaphorn's phone call found Lorenzo Perez at home, and Perez remembered Lieutenant Leaphorn.

"Hey," he said. "Hey, now. Talking to you takes me back a ways. You remember that time we caught that rustler that had rebuilt his house trailer so he could drive calves into it?"

Leaphorn remembered it, but he managed to steer Perez into the Halloween call. "They say you took the call on that one. It always seemed funny to me. Like more than a prank."

This produced a silence. Leaphorn cleared his throat. "Lorenzo. You still there?"

"I hope you're not just joking me," Perez said, sounding grim. "I've had enough of that."

"I'm not. I think something serious was going on out there that night."

"Well, I got joked about it, and made fun of, until I got just damn sick of it," Perez said. "I kept looking into it when I could. Kept trying to get the sheriff to get the army to do some sort of a general search. We didn't have the manpower to do it, of course, hundred and something thousand acres, lots of old empty buildings and damn near a thousand of those huge old bunkers. But the army could have done it. Would have, I'll bet you, if the sheriff had just got serious about it and made some sort of demand. But he just laughed. Said they didn't even have a missing person report. Nothing at all to go on."

"I'd like to talk to you about it," Leaphorn said.

They met at the coffee shop in the Gallup Mall.

Perez was one of those New Mexico Hispanics whose face suggests Castile and the Conquistadores more than Mexico. His gray hair was cut bristle-short, as was his mustache, and his very dark eyes examined Leaphorn as if looking for some sort of understanding.

"Driving over," he said, "I was thinking I don't know what I can tell you that's going to help whatever you're doing. I just talked to the kids that night, talked to them several other times, in fact, and kept going out there and nosing around. But I don't know how I can convince you that we had a murder, or something like it, committed out there that night."

Having said that, he picked up his menu, glanced at it, put it down, and shook his head. "I hate things I can't understand," he said.

"Me, too," Leaphorn said. He told Perez of his arrangement with Wiley Denton, of what the students he'd talked to had told him, and of his own hunch that Linda Denton might have been the wailing woman.

"About the only thing I can tell you that you might not know is that Wiley Denton told me he'd given Linda an expensive little disc player. One of those things with headphones that you carry around with you. When she left that morning to go to a lunch with some women friends, she took it with her."

"No," Perez said. "I didn't know that. The kids thought they heard music. At least Gracella Garcia did."

"And Mrs. Hano out at the Fort Wingate archives office told me McKay was out there that morning checking on something or other and that he had a woman in the car with him."

"Hey," said Perez, leaning forward. "Mrs. Denton?"

"She said she didn't know who it was. She just noticed a woman seemed to be sleeping in the car, and that McKay told her it was his wife."

"Did you check on that?"

"It wasn't McKay's wife," Leaphorn said. "She was at work in Gallup. McKay called her there."

"So he was lying to Mrs. Hano."

"So it would seem," Leaphorn said.

"Gracella was the one who seemed so certain about hearing music," Perez said. "A couple of the others thought it might have been the wind whistling, or maybe their imagination."

"I noticed that," Leaphorn said.

"She seemed like a pretty level-headed—" Perez stopped. "Wait a minute. When did Mrs. Hano talk to McKay? See the woman sleeping in his car?"

"About noon, I think," Leaphorn said. "I've got it in my notes."

"Gracella told me she'd noticed a car out there middle of the afternoon. She said they see army vehicles and trucks out there now and then, but this was a light-colored civilian sedan. What color was McKay's car?"

"I have no idea," Leaphorn said. "But I'll see if I can find out."

TWENTY-THREE

LEARNING THE COLOR of Marvin McKay's sedan proved to be so easy that Leaphorn found his whole attitude toward this dismal affair with Denton brightening. Deputy Price had told him no one had claimed McKay's few personal belongings. Not surprising since, aside from the few dollars in his wallet, they had little if any value. And then Price had described Peggy McKay as a common-law wife—which meant that, sans any proof of her relationship, getting personal items back would be complicated. But the car was another matter.

It had been parked at Denton's place, and it almost certainly remained parked there for days since this homicide wasn't one that received any normal criminal investigation. McKay wasn't charged with anything. His role was victim. Who cared about his car? Sooner or later, George Billie might have gotten tired of looking at it, called the sheriff, and had it towed away. Or maybe wired the ignition, drove it away himself, and sold it to the car strippers.

Leaphorn made another call to Denton's place.

"No," said Mrs. Mendoza, "he's still not home. Like I told you."

"Maybe you could help me, then," Leaphorn said. "Do you remember the car Mr. McKay drove? What color it was?"

"I don't pay much attention to cars," said Mrs. Mendoza, sounding out of patience.

"I just thought you might have remembered what color it was."

"Why don't you ask his lady about that car? I think she has it. Anyway, she came up here and drove it off."

"Well, thank you," Leaphorn said. "I will." And he put down the phone and sat a moment feeling stupid. Of course. There would be no reason for the police to impound that vehicle.

Judging from what he knew about McKay, the car was probably owned by Peggy. And judging from what he knew about public officials in general, there was no reason to believe anyone would have taken on the authority of having it towed into storage.

Peggy McKay answered the telephone on the first ring. Yes, she remembered Leaphorn, and yes, she had gotten a friend to drive her out to Denton's place to recover her car. What kind of car was it? A pale-blue Ford Escort. Yes, she still had it.

Leaphorn thought of the remarkable messiness of Mrs. McKay's house. "Do you know if the car has been through a car wash since your husband's death?"

Hesitation now, while Peggy McKay considered that.

"Not really," she said. "I hosed it off myself last spring after a muddy spell."

"I'd like to come over and take a look at it, if that's all right with you," Leaphorn said.

"Sure. Why not? I'll be home all day."

Just out of the driveway, he saw Louisa's car rolling up the street and stopped. So did she, and rolled down her window.

"I'm going into Gallup to talk to Mrs. McKay

again," he shouted. "Then maybe if he's home, I'll go see Denton."

"Why?"

"I want to tell him he's a liar and I don't want anything to do with him," Leaphorn said.

"Good for you," said Louisa. "And when you get back I've got some information for you."

"Like what?" Leaphorn said. But she had closed the window and was parking her car under her favorite tree across the street.

Peggy McKay hadn't bothered to park her Ford Escort in the shade. It sat in her drive, with its windows rolled down and its grimy pale-blue finish bearing evidence that it hadn't been through a car wash since its hosing last spring. Mrs. McKay appeared in her doorway as Leaphorn got out of his pickup.

"Feel free," she said, pointing to the car and laughing, "but don't get it dirty."

"Thanks," Leaphorn said.

"Have you had any luck? I mean, finding Mrs. Denton?"

"Not yet," Leaphorn said. He opened the passenger's-side door of the Escort. The interior reminded him of Mrs. McKay's living room.

"I'm not sure whether I told you," she said, coming down from the porch into her driveway. "I think Denton got off way too easy for shooting Marvin. I think it was a plain premeditated murder."

She was staring at Leaphorn, awaiting a response.

"The whole thing left a lot of unanswered questions," he said. And, when that didn't seem adequate, added: "Some pieces left out of the puzzle."

"What are you looking for in my car?"

"I guess you could say I'm just hoping to find one of the missing pieces."

"To find Linda Denton?"

"Yes," Leaphorn said.

"Not in that car, you won't," Mrs. McKay said. She walked back into her house and shut the door.

Leaphorn made another quick inspection of the front-seat area, looked into the back-seat space, opened the trunk of his own car and extracted the cardboard box he kept there to stash his grocery purchases and prevent them from rattling around. He put the box on the driveway and began extracting odds and ends from Mrs. McKay's floorboards—starting with a Baby Ruth wrapper, a crumpled tissue, a paper cup, a wrapper from a McDonald's hamburger, and a cigarette butt. Leaphorn inspected each item, at least with a glance, before adding it to his pile. By the time he had completed his search of both sides of the front seat and moved to the back, his box was almost half filled with wildly assorted trash, evidence that Mrs. McKay was a regular customer of various fast-food establishments and a person who saved Wal-Mart advertising sections, discount coupons, empty cigarette packages, and even the high heel from a black slipper. The only thing he found under the floor mats was a torn section from an Arizona road map, and it seemed to have no relevance.

Some of the stuff he set aside on a handkerchief he'd spread on the front seat—but very little. That included the quarter and dime he'd extracted from behind the passenger's-side seat, an assortment of long blonde hairs he'd carefully picked from under the passenger's-side headrest, a set of pliers he'd extracted from the glovebox, and a Chase Hardware sack and the sales slip he'd found crumpled inside it.

Leaphorn took time now to inspect the pliers and the slip. The slip had been issued the day before McKay was killed and covered the pliers (an expensive $24.95 set), a crowbar, and a roll of plumber's tape. He had found neither the tape nor the crowbar in the car. Leaphorn found himself imagining Linda Denton being hit on the head with one and bound with the other, and he made a mental note to ask Mrs. McKay about the purchases.

With the larger trash items out of the way, he removed the rear seat. Under it he found more trash, but nothing more interesting than an advertising flier for last year's Navajo Tribal Fair. Then he borrowed the flashlight from the glovebox, slid belly down onto the front floorboards, and pursued a close-up search there. The light and his probing hand harvested three business cards he'd missed (all from a State Farm Insurance salesman), a sock, another lost dime, what seemed to be a white marble but was actually a gum ball, a bright-red bead, and a small disk of clear glass that Leaphorn presumed at first was the lost face of a cheap watch.

He was wrong about that. When he held it up for inspection, he saw it was a lens. In fact, it was a progressive-focus lens prescribed and ground for those who need one focal length for reading, another for driving and other distances. Leaphorn slipped it into an envelope he saved from the trash, added the strands of hair, and sat awhile thinking. He was remembering one of the photographs on Wiley Denton's wall. Beautiful young Linda, her long blonde hair disheveled by the breeze, smiling at the photographer, wearing silver-rimmed glasses.

TWENTY-FOUR

LEAPHORN GAVE Mrs. McKay the coins, showed her the lens he'd found, asked her if she or any of her friends wore such glasses, and when she could think of none, he avoided her obvious question by refusing to speculate and saying he'd try to find out. Then he showed her the sales slip from the hardware store.

"Any idea what these were for?"

"What's this," Mrs. McKay said, peering at the slip. "Is that 'crowbar'?"

"That's the way I read it."

"We don't have one. I don't even know what it is."

"It's a steel bar with a sort of hook end used for prying things," Leaphorn said. "How about the other items?"

"I can hardly believe it," she said, and laughed. "We have a drip under the sink. For months we had a drip, and Marvin said not to worry, he'd fix it. I guess he finally got around to it." But as she tried to go on, her voice broke. She looked away. "I mean, I guess he was going to."

Leaphorn had intended to borrow Mrs. McKay's telephone to call home, but grief prefers privacy. He drove out to a motel parking lot on old U.S. 66 and called his Window Rock number from the pay phone. Louisa answered.

"Are you at Wiley Denton's house?" she asked.

"Not yet," he said. "That's my next stop."

"He's in oil and gas leases, that sort of thing, isn't he? If he is, ask him if he knows anything about the ownership of Mock Land and Cattle Company or Apache Pipe."

"What's up?" Leaphorn asked. "I think that cattle company is Bill Mock's outfit. Or used to be. Probably owned by his heirs now. He operated a good-sized feedlot operation in Sandoval County, and a ranch."

"Feedlot?"

"Where buyers fatten up range cattle before they send them off to become sirloins and hamburgers," Leaphorn said. "And Apache Pipe, I think that's Denton. Years ago, he went into it with the Jicarilla tribe to finance the gas-collection system for the gas wells, but I heard he bought out the tribe's interest."

"Denton's," said Louisa. "How about that."

"Tell me," Leaphorn said.

"That land on top of Mesa de los Lobos is the typical Checkerboard Reservation jumble, which won't surprise you. Much of the north slope of the mesa is reserved Navajo land, and a lot of the south side was in the allocation the government gave to the railroad. Some of that somehow went back into public domain ownership—probably some swapping back and forth with private ownership, and you Navajos bought back a piece of it, and other chunks were sold off by the railroad to various private owners. I'll guess you knew a lot of that already."

"Some of it," Leaphorn said.

"The parcel I think you and Sergeant Chee might be interested in is a six-section block at the head of the Coyote Canyon drainage. Somebody named Arthur Sanders and Sons bought it from the outfit handling land sales for the railroad in 1878. That must have become Sanders Cattle, because in 1903 William L. Elrod bought it from them. Since then, there's two more transfers of title, looks like due to deaths and inheritances, but the company with the title to the six sections is still Elrod Land and Cattle Company. You got that?"

"I've got it," Leaphorn said. "I imagine Chee will want to find out if the Elrod people know what's going on down at the bottom end of their canyon. And thanks. This must have been a lot of hard work for you."

"Hold it. Hold it," Louisa said. "I haven't got to the hard-work part yet, where it gets complicated."

"Oh?"

"Elrod also has a grazing lease on a small tract of Bureau of Land Management land adjoining its property. There's some sort of legal question about whether that lease will be renewed. Argument over whether Elrod overgrazed it, I think it is. Anyway, Elrod dropped its application to renew on that, and the existing lease expires September one."

"September one," Leaphorn said. "Couple more weeks to run then. Any significance to that?"

"I don't know, but maybe. There's an option to buy, contract to sell recorded, which is tied to the Bureau of Land Management lease. Effective when the lease expires. The clerk at the BLM office said Apache would probably apply for the lease, but hasn't yet. She said the little tract is just a sort of cut-off corner, and she didn't think anyone else would want it."

"The purchase price didn't happen to be on the record?"

"They never are," Louisa said.

"Let's see," Leaphorn said. "Six sections at six hundred forty acres per section would be almost four thousand acres. With dry country grazing land close to worthless, I doubt if the price would matter to Denton."

Louisa laughed. "Not for raising cattle anyway. The BLM was calculating you could graze eight units per square mile on it. I guess that's eight cows per section."

"Cow plus its calf," Leaphorn said.

"So I guess that you guess that Mr. Denton

isn't buying it for grazing calves. He thinks he can find the old Golden Calf gold mine up there. Am I right about that?"

"Almost," Leaphorn said. "I think he found the Golden Calf a long time ago."

"Did something you found out today tell you that? Come on home and tell me about it."

"I will," Leaphorn said. "But now I've got to go see Wiley Denton and let him know I'm calling off any sort of arrangement he thinks we might have."

Louisa took a moment to think about this.

"Joe," she said. "I think you should be very careful with this Denton. Don't you think he must be kind of crazy?"

"I have been thinking that for quite a while," Leaphorn said.

TWENTY-FIVE

LEAPHORN'S NEXT CALL was to Wiley Denton's unlisted number. Mrs. Mendoza answered. Yes, Mr. Denton was now home.

"You finding anything useful?" Denton asked. "And how about giving me some sort of idea how much you're charging me?"

"I'll be out to your place in about thirty minutes," Leaphorn said. "I have something I want to show you."

"Well, how much are you going to charge me?"

"Absolutely nothing," Leaphorn said, and hung up.

George Billie was standing by the garage

door as Leaphorn stopped at the entry gate. The entry gate slid open, smooth and silent.

"He said to bring you right in," Billie said after Leaphorn parked his car. Billie held the door open and led Leaphorn down the long carpeted hallway to the office. Denton was sitting behind his desk, staring at Leaphorn, his expression blank.

"I guess we're even on the 'hanging up the telephone on one another' business," Denton said. "But at least you didn't call me a son of a bitch."

"No," Leaphorn said. "But I'm going to call you a liar."

Denton's only reaction to that was to continue the stare and, finally, to scratch his ear.

"Maybe I'll make that a damned liar," Leaphorn said.

"I guess I've done a little of that," Denton said. "This oil-leasing business sometimes requires it. But now you're going to tell me what you found. And how badly you're going to rip me off when you bill me for your services."

"I found this," Leaphorn said. He took the envelope from his shirt pocket, extracted the lens, held it out toward Denton on his finger.

Denton stared at it, frowned. Said, "What

is—" Then he leaned back in his chair, eyes closed, his face a mask of tense muscles. "A lens," he said. "Is that from Linda's glasses?"

"I don't know," Leaphorn said, and held it out. "Do you think it is?"

Denton let out a long-held breath, opened his eyes, leaned forward, and held out his hand. Leaphorn put the lens on his palm. Denton picked it up with finger and thumb, very gently, studied it, held it up to the light, and looked through it for a long moment. Then he laid it carefully on the desk blotter.

"She had beautiful eyes," he said. "Blue as the sky. Most beautiful eyes I ever saw."

Leaphorn said nothing. Denton's own eyes were watering, and then he was crying. He didn't wipe the tears away. No more tension in his face now, but he looked terribly old.

"Where'd you find her?" he asked.

"I didn't find her," Leaphorn said. "I found the lens under the front seat of the car McKay was driving the day you killed him."

"Just that?"

"That's all, and a few long blonde hairs caught in the passenger-side front-seat headrest. Peggy McKay has black hair."

"That bastard," Denton said. "That sick son

of a bitch." He rubbed the back of his hand across his face, got up, and walked to the window. He looked out for a moment, then back at Leaphorn. "She had her hair fixed real pretty when she left that morning for that lunch party she was going to. Or said she was going to."

"And she was wearing her glasses?"

"She always did," Denton said, returning his gaze out the window. "I wanted to get her fitted with some of those contact lenses you wear right on your eyes, but she said she never could read well with them on. And she was reading all the time."

"I hear that's common," Leaphorn said.

"She was far-sighted," Denton said in a choked voice. "Said she just needed longer arms." He forced what sounded a little like a chuckle. "But she said the ones she had were long enough to wrap around me."

"It sounds like you're certain that lens is from Linda's glasses."

"Yeah. What else," Denton said, still looking at whatever attracted him outside. "It's the same oval shape. One of those merged-in trifocal grinds."

"Let's go back to where we started," Leaphorn said. "Get back to that day you asked me if I would look for your wife. See if I could find what happened to her, anyway. And I said I would if you wouldn't lie to me. You've been lying to me, so I'm quitting. But I'd still like some straight answers out of you."

Denton had turned away from the window. "Lying about what?" The bright backlighting from the window made it impossible for Leaphorn to read his expression, but the tone was hostile.

"About the maps, for starters. McKay wasn't trying to sell you a location in the Zuñi Mountains. His was on Mesa de los Lobos. Then there's the circumstances of how you shot him. He wasn't just leaving when that happened. He was—"

"What makes you think that?"

"McKay was a sort of fancy dresser. He wouldn't have been walking out of here without his expensive leather jacket, which was hanging on that chair over there with no bullet hole in it, and no blood."

Denton walked over and sat behind his desk, studying Leaphorn. He shrugged. "So what?" he said. "Whether he was leaving, or just getting ready to leave."

"Then there's the gun. Big, clumsy long-barrel thirty-eight revolver. He wouldn't have been carrying a gun like that in the pocket of his jacket. It wouldn't fit anyway. Hell of a job to get it in your pants pocket. Or out of it."

Denton shrugged again. "You're sounding like a damned lawyer."

"Peggy McKay says he didn't have a gun."

Now Denton leaned forward. "What are you saying? You saying I just shot the bastard down and planted the gun on him? Like you police sometimes do?"

"Something like that. Am I close?"

A long minute of silence followed that question. Leaphorn remembered Louisa's warning to him to be careful—that Denton might be a little crazy. He'd always figured Denton to be a little crazy. Who wasn't? But he was conscious of how Denton had moved behind the desk, of desk drawers with pistols in them.

Denton had come to some sort of decision. He exhaled, shook his head, said: "What you're suggesting is I had that pistol in here all ready to plant on him. You're suggesting I invited him here just to execute him. Right? Now why in the world would I do that? The

man's trying to sell me what I've been trying
to buy. The location of the Golden Calf."

"Because," Leaphorn said, and hesitated.
Perhaps it was time for him to lie himself.
Time to avoid standing right where Marvin
McKay had stood. But he was already past
that point. "Because you already knew where
this legendary gold deposit is located. You'd
already found it. When you learned McKay
knew the location, you didn't want him
around spreading the word."

"Hell," Denton said. "That doesn't make
much sense, does it? Why would I give a damn
if he talked about it? People been talking
about finding the Golden Calf for a hundred
years. More than that. And nobody would believe them. Why would they believe a con
artist? And why would I care anyway?"

"Because at the end of the month, an option
you have with Elrod Land and Cattle to buy
that land at the head of Coyote Canyon goes
into effect," Leaphorn said. "If the word gets
out before then, the deal can be canceled."

Denton's swivel chair creaked as he leaned
back in it, studying Leaphorn. His hands were
out of sight, under the table. Then the left one

reappeared. He rubbed the crooked hump of his broken nose. Made a wry face.

"Where'd you hear that?"

"It's public record," Leaphorn said. "The contract's tied in with the Bureau of Land Management lease."

"So what," Denton said. "What if you're guessing right? So you think that gives me a motive for murder. Hell, man, I've already been to court on this thing. Found guilty of killing McKay. Already served my time in prison. You know the law. It's over with. No double jeopardy. And what's any of this have to do with finding Linda? That's what you're supposed to be doing."

"That brings us to one of your deceptions that has a lot to do with finding Linda. Let's see if you'll tell the truth about that."

Denton produced a hostile grin. "It's deception now, is it, instead of lie? Well, go ahead. Let's hear it."

"Before McKay came out here that evening he called his wife. Told her he was bringing you your map and all that. He said that from the questions you'd been asking him, he thought you might be planning to cheat him.

Take the map and his information and not give him the fifty thousand. He said in case that happened, he had a back-up plan, insurance, something to make you pay."

"She told you that, did she?"

"She did, and with nothing to gain from lying about it."

"What was this insurance? This back-up plan?"

"You tell me," Leaphorn said. "McKay didn't tell her what he had in mind. So now you tell me what he said. It might help us find your wife."

Denton said nothing. He looked away from Leaphorn, at the window. When he looked back, the bravado had slipped away. He shook his head.

"I don't know."

"Come on, Denton, stop wasting our time," Leaphorn said. "You know now Linda must have been in McKay's car out at Fort Wingate that afternoon. That would have been just before he came here. Just before he called his own wife and told her about his 'insurance.' Why not quit kidding yourself?"

Denton had lowered his head into his

hands, and was shaking it back and forth. He didn't look up. "Shut up," he said. "Shut up, damn you, and get out of here. And don't ever come back."

TWENTY-SIX

LORENZO PEREZ was in his front yard holding a garden hose with a high-pressure nozzle when Leaphorn drove up—and was doing what seemed eccentric to Leaphorn.

"Watering your rosebush?" he asked. "Looks like you're trying to knock the leaves off."

"No," said Perez, "I'm trying to get rid of the damned aphids."

"They don't like water?"

Perez laughed. "You try to knock them off the stems," Perez said. "It's better than using poison. That kills the ladybugs, and the birds, and all your other helpers. If you can knock the aphids off with the water, they can't climb back up again." He turned off the hose. "But it's a lost cause anyway, trying to grow roses in Gallup. Wrong climate."

"I need a favor, if you have time."

"When you catch me out squirting water on aphids, you know I'm not terrible busy."

"I'm still on that wailing woman business out at the fort," Leaphorn said. "I wanted to see if you could give me a clearer picture of just where those kids were when they heard it, and from which direction they said the sounds were coming."

"You mean go on out there and sort of try to re-create it for you?"

"That's what I had in mind. And maybe see if we could get Gracella Garcia to come along."

"I guess we could handle that. When you want to do it?"

"How about right now?"

"I can't do it today," Perez said. "You in a hurry?"

"Sort of," said Leaphorn. "But I guess it could wait."

"I could pretty well tell you just where it was, if you're in a rush," said Perez as he walked over to his fence. "You know they have those bunkers blocked off? Well, they were—"

"Well, no, I don't. I never had very much business out there, and when I did I wasn't paying that sort of attention."

"You know the military, though," Perez said. "The army divided all those bunkers off into ten blocks, and lettered the blocks from A to J, and then numbered the bunkers. Like, for example, B1028."

"Divided them off by what they had in them?" Leaphorn asked.

"God knows," Perez said. "I think they did it during the Vietnam War when they added some new ones. They were running virtually all the munitions and explosive stuff through Wingate then. Busy, busy. Artillery shells, rockets, mines, everything. Big boom for Gallup. New rail lines had to be built, everything." Perez laughed. "They even built concrete shelters every so often so people working could run in them for shelter in case lightning might strike something and blow things up."

Leaphorn had stopped paying close attention to the rest of this report after Perez cited the bunker-labeling system.

"Each bunker had its own number?"

"Letter and number."

"How many bunkers in each block?"

"I don't know. They used ten letters, A through J, and there's about eight hundred bunkers, so I'd guess a hundred to a block, but maybe they lettered 'em by what's stored inside. Like 'A' for artillery, and 'B' for bombs, and—" Perez paused, unable to think of anything that exploded that started with a "C." "These days, 'E' for empty would be the letter they'd need for most of the blocks. Anyway, the army rule was no bunker could be closer than two hundred yards to another one, and they used about twenty-four-thousand acres scattering them out. Had to build a hell of a lot of railroad track."

"How about the numbers?" Leaphorn asked. "I noticed some of them had four numbers after the letter."

Perez frowned. "I think maybe all of them did," he said. "No idea why, except they seemed to be in order. Like B1222 would come after B1221."

"What block were the kids in?"

"I think it was 'D,'" Perez said. "Or maybe 'C.'"

"I'm going on out there and look around,"

Leaphorn said. "If I learn anything, I'll call you."

But now Leaphorn found he couldn't remember the number on the card with Doherty's stuff. He was sure it began with a D, but his usually fine memory had jumbled together Peshlakai's cell phone number, Denton's unlisted number, his advertisement number, and Doherty's four digits. But he did remember telling the number to Chee, and Chee jotting it into his notebook.

Chee was probably still in Gallup. Leaphorn called the FBI office there. Chee wasn't there, but Bernie was. She said Chee would be in any minute for a meeting with Osborne. Did he want to leave a message?

"I wanted to ask him if he had that number found on the back of that business card in Doherty's stuff. I remember he wrote it down."

"It was a 'D' followed by 2187," she said. "Have you found out what it's about?"

"It's probably the number of a bunker out at Fort Wingate," Leaphorn said, thinking how great it had been when he, too, had had such a young and vigorous memory. He explained as much as he knew of the army's blocking system.

"Something to do with the old McKay homicide, you think? Something to do with that wailing woman business?"

"I don't know," Leaphorn said. "I'm going on out there now and see if I can find a bunker with that number on it. And I thought Jim or you might want to check on it."

"You bet," Bernie said. "And by the way, Mr. Denton called for you here. He said he needed to find you as soon as he could. He said it was urgent. He wanted you to call him."

"Did he say why?"

"I asked. He wouldn't tell me."

Mrs. Mendoza answered the telephone at the Denton home, confirmed that Mr. Denton wanted to talk to him, and put him through.

"Leaphorn," Denton said. "Are you still in Gallup? Come on out to the house. I've got something I have to tell you. Something important."

"I don't work for you anymore, Mr. Denton," Leaphorn said. "In fact, I never did work for you."

"To hell with that," Denton said. "This is something you really need to know."

"Then tell me."

"Not on the damned telephone. I think the

FBI has had this line tapped because of the Doherty case. They think I'm involved in that. Come on out."

"I learned in all these years as a cop that when somebody has something important to tell me, it turns out to be a lot more important to them than it is to me."

Silence. Then Denton said, "Meet me half-way then. Where are you?"

Leaphorn considered that. "All right," he said. "In fifteen minutes from now I'll pull into the parking lot at the Smith grocery on Railroad Avenue. You remember my pickup truck?"

"I do," Denton said. "I'll be there."

And there he was, sitting in his big, mud-splattered off-road sports utility vehicle watching as Leaphorn made his turn into the lot, getting out and walking over as Leaphorn parked, leaning in the passenger's-side window.

"Let's take your truck," he said.

"Take it where?" Leaphorn asked.

"Someplace quiet where I can tell you my secret," Denton said while he opened the door and got in.

Leaphorn wasn't liking any of this. He had

the uneasy feeling he'd miscalculated.

"We'll do our talking here," Leaphorn said.

"No," Denton said, shaking his head. "Let's get away from all these people."

"Just tell me this secret of yours," Leaphorn said. "Not that I guarantee I'll believe it."

"Part of the secret is I may have to kill you," Denton said, and he pressed what felt like the barrel of a pistol against Leaphorn's ribs.

TWENTY-SEVEN

WHEN DEALING with federal agencies, Sergeant Jim Chee was always conscious of the "Navajo time" stereotype applied to the Dineh. Thus he showed up at the Gold Avenue address of the FBI ten minutes early. Bernie was in the entrance area talking to the receptionist as Chee passed through the metal detector. She looked, as usual, slightly disheveled, as if some impossible breeze had invaded this guarded office, ruffled her hair, and moved the collar of her uniform shirt slightly out of its official alignment. With that notion of her thus confirmed by his glance, Chee's analysis and conclusions advanced to another level. Officer

Bernadette Manuelito was a very bewitching young woman in a way he couldn't quite define. Certainly Bernadette's style was equal to (and far beyond) the perfect beauty of Janet Pete or the sensuous, soft, blonde charms of Mary Landon. With that established, and just as Bernie noticed his arrival and turned and recognized him with a smile, Sergeant Chee's consciousness took the great jump to the very top level. Face it. He had fallen in love with Officer Manuelito. And what the devil could he do about that?

Bernie's welcoming smile faded into a wry look.

"The meeting's been postponed," she said. "Something came up down at the Zuñi Pueblo, and the Albuquerque Office supervisor came in, and now Osborne has to go down there with them."

Chee said: "Oh, well." Which wasn't what he would have said had he not been suddenly engulfed with a flood of thoughts about Bernadette Manuelito. "So what?" he added.

"And," Bernie added, "Lieutenant Leaphorn called for you here. He wanted to ask you the number that was on a card with Mr. Doherty's stuff."

"Number?" Chee said. "What number?"

"The number was D2187," Bernie said. "Don't you remember? It was written on the back of a business card Doherty had, and nobody had any idea what it was about."

"Oh," Chee said. "I remember telling Leaphorn about it. I thought he might understand it. Has the Legendary Lieutenant now solved the number puzzle?"

"He thinks it's the army's munitions depot code number for one of the bunkers out at Fort Wingate," Bernie said. Chee was just standing there, staring at her with a strange look on his face but no sign of understanding.

"He thinks it might be near where those kids heard the wailing woman the night Mr. McKay was killed," Bernie said, wondering what was bothering Chee.

"Oh," Chee said. "He wanted me to call him? Where? I need to call him anyway about talking to Hostiin Peshlakai this morning. About what Peshlakai said."

"Maybe at Mr. Denton's place. He said he had to see Denton about something. But he also said he was going out to the fort to see what he could find out," Bernie said. "And what did Hostiin Peshlakai tell you?"

"It's complicated," Chee said. "Let's find Leaphorn first."

He called Denton's number. No, Mrs. Mendoza said, Leaphorn wasn't there and neither was Mr. Denton. "I heard them talking on the telephone. I think Mr. Denton drove down into Gallup to meet him somewhere."

"Let's go find Leaphorn at the fort," Chee said. "I'll tell you on the way out."

"You sound nervous," Bernie said.

"I am," Chee said. "From what Peshlakai told me, I think our Legendary Lieutenant is playing with fire."

TWENTY-EIGHT

AS HE ROLLED his truck through the grocery parking lot toward the exit, Leaphorn was analyzing his situation. It didn't seem reasonable to believe that Wiley Denton actually intended to kill him. However, there was a lot of circumstantial evidence that suggested otherwise. For one thing, he had given Denton a motive. Louisa had warned him that Denton was dangerous. He'd already known that. And yet Leaphorn had unloaded on the man the very evidence Denton had already killed one man—and probably two—to protect. He had poked Denton's two sorest spots—his obsess-

sion to claim the Golden Calf, legendary or
not, and his desperate love of his missing wife.

At this tense moment, Leaphorn was doubt-
ing his judgment on several things, but not on
that. Denton dearly loved the girl who had
been willing to marry him. Leaphorn had
been a fool for love himself, had been there
and done that, would never ever forget
Emma. He crept through the parking-lot traffic, giving right-of-way to everyone, thinking
about tactics.

"Move along," Denton said, pushing the pistol against Leaphorn's side. "Do a left turn out
on Railroad Avenue."

"You were going to tell me something I
needed to know," Leaphorn said. "Remember? Called it a secret. That's how you got me
to meet you."

"We'll get to that when we get where we
have some privacy."

"Give me a hint," Leaphorn said. "Tell me
what McKay told you about his back-up plan.
No use to keep lying, is there?"

Denton snorted. "You're not going to believe this, either."

"Probably not," Leaphorn said. "Why not try

me?" He stopped again and waved ahead a blue Chevy that was waiting for him to pass.

"All right," Denton said. "McKay said he had a love affair started with Linda, but she didn't want to leave me. So he made this bet with her. He took her to a little hut way back in the Zuñi Mountains. Took her shoes away from her, and said he was going back to see me and tell me I could have her back along with his Golden Calf map for fifty thousand dollars."

The Chevy drove past. The pickup behind Leaphorn honked.

"What else did he say?"

"He said he bet her I wouldn't pay to get her back."

The pickup honked again. Leaphorn eased his truck forward.

"What'd you say to that?"

Denton's laugh had a bitter sound. "Just like the court records show. Marvin McKay pulled out his pistol, and I shot the son of a bitch."

Leaphorn was heading for the exit now, a bit above the legal pace. "Didn't you believe him?"

"Of course not," Denton said.

"How about now?"

"Well, maybe some of it. Do a left on Railroad."

Leaphorn jammed down on the accelerator and made a tire-squealing right turn into a gap in the traffic. He felt the pistol barrel jamming into his ribs.

"Left," Denton said. "We're going the wrong way."

"We're going the right way," Leaphorn said. "And I don't think you're going to shoot me because I think you still want me to find Linda for you."

"Fat chance of that," Denton said. But the pistol moved away from Leaphorn's ribs. "What do you mean?"

"I mean, I think I know where she is, and I want to go there and find out. But first, I've got to make a telephone call."

Denton laughed. "Oh, come on, Leaphorn. You've been calling me a liar, but you never called me stupid before."

"I call Lorenzo Perez; he calls the security man at Fort Wingate and tells him we've got business out in the bunker area and to let us in."

"Fort Wingate?" Denton said. "You said McKay was there the day I shot him, and he had a woman in his car. Right?"

Leaphorn nodded.

"Who's this Perez?"

"Former undersheriff. Knows people at the fort. Hand me the cell phone out of the glovebox."

Denton got out the cell phone, inspected it, said: "What's the number for Perez?"

Leaphorn told him.

"You know how it sounds when you cock a pistol?"

"Sure."

"Then listen to this." The click of a pistol being cocked followed. "The pistol is a forty-five caliber. You know what that does to somebody. If you say anything to Perez that sounds suspicious to me, then I shoot you, turn off the ignition, grab the wheel, pull your truck off the road, wipe everything down for my fingerprints, leave the gun on the floor. No prints on it and none on the rounds in the magazine. There'll be not a drop of blood on me. I just open the door and step out and walk away."

"You won't have to bother with a self-defense plea this time, then," Leaphorn said.

"Right," said Denton. He pushed the speaker volume to the top, dialed the number, listened for a second to the voice that answered, then handed it to Leaphorn.

"Lorenzo, this is Joe Leaphorn. Can I get you to call security out at Fort Wingate and ask them to let me in? Just tell 'em I'm working on something with you."

"Sure," Lorenzo said. "I already did. What is—"

"Thanks," Leaphorn said, and disconnected.

"Already did?" Denton said. "What's that mean?"

"I told him I was going out there today to see what I could find."

Denton didn't comment on that. And when Leaphorn asked him what else McKay had said about Linda and his back-up plan, Denton said, "I don't want to talk about it." The rest of the trip was made in tense and gloomy silence. Leaphorn broke it once, just before they made the turn into the fort's entrance, to comment on a massive cumulus-nebulous cloud building up over the Zuñi Mountains. He pointed toward it. "Maybe we'll finally get some rain," he said. "That looks promising."

Denton said, "Just drive," and he didn't

speak again until Leaphorn slowed at the security gate of the bunker area.

"Remember this," he said, and showed Leaphorn the pistol, one of those 1902 model .45 automatics the U.S. Army had been using through every war up to Desert Storm. "If the security man at the gate wants to talk, don't."

The security man offered no opportunity for conversation. He simply grinned and waved them through.

Leaphorn had long since abandoned the notion that Wiley Denton wouldn't actually shoot him and had been concentrating on coming up with some sort of action to abort that. He'd read too much and had seen too many movies about the training of the Green Berets in efficient killing to have much hope of overpowering Denton. He might be rusty, being half a lifetime away from ambushing Vietcong on the Cambodian side of the Ho Chi Minh Trail, but he was incurably bigger, burlier, and, alas, younger than Leaphorn. He'd finally settled on getting Denton to bunker D2187 so filled with dread (or hope) concerning what they might find there that he would be—despite his training—incautious for a required moment or two. During which Leaphorn would do something suitable, which he hoped he could think of.

Now, however, the problem was finding bunker D2187 in the vast maze of weed-grown railroad tracks, crumbling asphalt access roads, and rows and rows of great grassy humps. While these were neatly spaced two hundred yards apart as the army had required, the rolling terrain of the Zuñi Mountains foothills defeated the West Pointian obsession with straight and unbroken lines. After two wrong turns, one of which led them into an old but still unbroken security fence, Denton began to lose patience.

"I'm beginning to get skeptical about this," he said. "Where do you think you're going?"

"We're going to a block of bunkers labeled 'D,'" Leaphorn said.

"These have a 'G' over the doors," Denton said. "Are you lost, or are you just bulling me?"

Leaphorn backed around, made the first possible right turn onto a street where the asphalt paving was so worn it was mostly reduced to gravel. The first bunker he passed bore the label D2163 (faded by years of weather) over its massive door. After a slow quarter mile of counting off numbers, Leaphorn pulled his pickup off the gravel and parked in front of bunker D2187. Finally! It actually existed. He took a deep breath and blew it out.

"This is it?" Denton asked.

Leaphorn took his flashlight from the glovebox, opened his door, got out, and studied the bunker door—a great, heavy slab of steel covered with peeled and rusty-looking army paint. Fastened to the bunker's bare cement front to the right of the entry were two steel boxes, mounted side by side, labeled, respectively, "1" and "2." A metal tube ran up the concrete face of the bunker into box 2, and another such tube linked box 2 to box 1, from which five similar tubes emerged. One ran up the face of the bunker and disappeared over the roof. The four others ran downward, three of them disappearing through the front of the bunker at floor level and the other running along the ground and up the wall and linking to a device on one of the bottom hinges.

Denton had now joined him in this inspection.

"The one going over the roof probably served the ventilating pump they have on top of these bunkers," Denton said. "The others probably involve some sort of an alarm system, humidity or temperature sensors, or maybe an alarm to signal if the door opened without the proper code." He produced a contemptuous snort. "And you haven't got the code."

"Nobody has the code," Leaphorn said. "It's been decommissioned for years. The army base up in Utah that is supposed to keep an eye on things uses it now and then to shoot off target rockets down to White Sands for that Star Wars foolishness. No need for security anymore."

As he was explaining that, he was thinking the door seemed altogether too secure. Another steel box, slightly rusted, was welded to its center. Near the bottom was a bolt locking device. The bolt seemed to be missing. The only thing Leaphorn was sure he understood was the steel locking bar that swung across the door and, when clamped down, prevented it from being opened.

Leaphorn took two steps toward the door.

"Hold it," Denton said. "You want me to believe you're going to get into that vault?"

Denton was holding the .45, still cocked, now pointed at the ground about halfway between him and Leaphorn.

"We'll see," Leaphorn said, and walked to the door.

It wasn't a fast walk. Leaphorn had become belatedly aware that he had managed to make himself an ally to Denton if Denton planned to kill him and get away with it. The thunderstorm brewing over the Zuñis was producing lightning now and would probably dump enough rain to erase their tracks. The rumble of thunder echoed along the rows of bunkers, and the updrafts feeding the cloud were producing gusty winds. He had brought Denton to an absolutely perfect place for Denton to shoot him. No one would be near enough to hear a pistol shot even on a quiet day. Denton could probably drive out through the main gate with no more than a wave, or if he thought the security man would be curious, he could find a way out easily enough on the Zuñi Mountains side, where ranchers had been using their wire cutters for years to get their cattle into the free grazing.

Now that he was closer, Leaphorn could read the faded little sign posted over the box on the door: LOCK DOOR. Bad news. He checked the small box on the door, which he now saw was like those used in prisons as containers for coded locking devices. But, good news, this box was empty.

Then he noticed at his feet a section of thick wire. He picked it up. It had been cut. Still on the wire was a circular metal tab. Leaphorn found the place where the wire had been run through a flange on the door and a matching flange on the doorjamb. This tab had been the official seal.

"Okay, Leaphorn," Denton said. "Enough of this screwing around. I think this is a sort of setup. You're killing time. Waiting for somebody to come."

It was just then that Leaphorn remembered both the pliers and the crowbar. McKay had used the pliers to cut the wire. As he looked at the metal locking bar in place across the door, he understood why McKay had bought the crowbar. He needed it as a "cheat bar," to apply leverage to push the blocking bar up out of the slots that held it. But what had McKay done with it? He'd found the pliers in McKay's car. Once the wire was cut, he had no more need for them here. But if he'd left Linda Denton locked in this bunker, he'd need the crowbar to get her out.

Denton was standing right behind Leaphorn now, and he pressed the pistol against Leaphorn's spine.

"Back in the truck," he said. "Now, or I kill you here."

As he heard that, Leaphorn saw the crowbar, lying in the weeds against the concrete wall.

He pointed to it.

"Marvin McKay bought that bar at a Gallup hardware store the day you killed him," Leaphorn said. "Put that damned pistol back in your pocket, and we'll pick up the crowbar and use it to find out what happened to your wife."

Again, the pressure of the pistol against Leaphorn's back disappeared.

"What are you talking about?" Denton said.

"I'm getting the crowbar. I'll show you."

Leaphorn picked up the heavy steel bar and examined the locking arrangement a moment. Using the flange as a fulcrum, he put the bar end under the locking bar and pulled down with his full weight. The locking bar slid upward.

"Now, pull the door open."

Denton did.

They stood engulfed in a rush of warm, stale air, and peered into a vast, empty darkness. Nothing but a clutter of cartons against the left wall, and two black barrel-like containers that once had probably held some sort of explosive. Denton was holding the pistol down by his side now.

"You think she's in there?"

The only light in the bunker followed them through the doorway. It dimly illuminated a gray concrete floor, which stretched sixty empty feet to the great half circle of gray concrete that formed the back wall.

Leaphorn walked in just a few steps before he noticed Denton wasn't following. He was still standing, slumped, staring at the door post.

"What'd you find?" Leaphorn said, and walked back toward the door.

Denton pointed, but his eyes were closed.

Words were scrawled on the concrete. Leaphorn turned on his flashlight and illuminated: BUMP I AM SO SORRY.

"You know who this 'Bump' is?"

"I'm Bump," Denton said. "Because of my nose." He touched a finger to the disfigurement.

"Oh," Leaphorn said.

"She said she loved that bump on my nose. That it reminded her of the kind of man I was." Denton tried to laugh at that, but couldn't manage it. "Had to be Linda who wrote it," he said. "Nobody else called me that."

Leaphorn touched the scrawl. "I think she must have written this with her lipstick," he said.

"I'll go find her," Denton said. "Linda," he shouted, and rushed off into the gloom with the shout echoing and echoing in the huge empty tomb.

They found Mrs. Linda Denton, née Linda Verbiscar, lying primly on a sheet of heavy corrugated cardboard behind the empty drums.

She was facedown, with her head turned sideways. The cool, utterly dry, almost airless climate of the sealed bunker had converted her into a mummy.

TWENTY-NINE

WHAT HOSTIIN PESHLAKAI had told Chee, he had recited in the presence of Ms. Knoblock, his court-appointed attorney, and Mr. Harjo, who seemed to be serving as her interpreter as well as Agent Osborne's. And Peshlakai spoke, as seemed to be his habit, in general and ambiguous terms.

"But what it all boiled down to, Bernie, when you read between the lines, and you went ahead and completed a few sentences for him, was that Wiley Denton murdered Doherty with our friend Peshlakai aiding and abetting—if not actually pulling the trigger."

Bernie looked very sad when she heard

that. "Putting that old man in prison," she said. "That would be awful. That would kill him."

"Probably," Chee said. "But I don't think Harjo actually understood a lot of it. Not from the way he was translating it to Ms. Knoblock."

Bernie gave him a sidelong glance. "And you didn't butt in and explain things to them. Right? You seem to be implying something, well, something sneaky."

"I don't know what I'm implying," Chee said. "But I know for sure that Peshlakai had no idea he was getting himself involved in a murder."

"How did he get tied up with Denton anyway?"

"Just by living where he did. He'd see Denton coming up the canyon, nosing around, digging out sand samples and that sort of thing. And he must have warned Denton that he shouldn't go up to the headwaters area of Coyote Canyon because of the holy places there. He would be violating taboos, and that would make him sick. And so Denton was sympathetic, or seemed to be, and said he'd help Peshlakai guard the place. Denton gave Peshlakai a cell phone, showed him how to use it, and told him when he saw anyone prowling around up the canyon, he should call."

"So he called him when Doherty showed up at the placer site?"

"Exactly," Chee said. "And Denton came. Whereupon one of them shot Doherty."

"With Peshlakai's rifle?"

"Unfortunately. Peshlakai didn't say so, but Osborne's crime scene crew finally recovered the slug with their metal detectors. It matched that old thirty-thirty, just like the bullet he fired to scare you away."

Bernie shuddered, remembering that. "And they put Doherty's body back in his truck," Bernie said. "And then one of them drove it up to where I found it, and the other one came along in Denton's car, and then everybody went home. Everybody except Thomas Doherty."

"Peshlakai didn't get into explaining that, or say who actually fired the shot."

Bernie sighed. "I don't guess it matters much. Whether he's killer or conspirator. He's way too old to last long in prison."

"He wouldn't want to," Chee said.

Bernie rubbed her hand across her face. "I

hate this," she said. "Just hate it. So many people get hurt."

"I know," Chee said. A long silence followed. Chee broke it with what sounded a little like a laugh.

"What?" Bernie said.

"I sounded like I was agreeing with you, but I really wasn't. You were feeling pity for the victims, and sometimes the ones we arrest are the worst victims of all. I wasn't thinking that. I was thinking about us."

"What do you mean?"

"You might have been killed in Coyote Canyon," Chee said. "That's been a nightmare ever since you told me."

"No one would have blamed you for it," Bernie said.

"I didn't mean that," Chee said.

They turned into the fort entrance, showed their police credentials at the security gate, were assured that Leaphorn and another man had driven through a bit earlier, and were given some general instructions about how to find the D block of bunkers and bunker D2187.

Bernie spotted Leaphorn's pickup far ahead as they turned onto the worn asphalt lane, and they parked behind it.

"The door's open," Bernie said.

Chee took out his flashlight and stepped out of the car. Bernie was already out.

"Bernie. Why don't you wait here until I—"

"Because I'm a cop, just as much as you are."

"But I'm the sergeant," Chee said. "Stay back."

He walked to the open door, looked in, flicked on his flashlight.

The beam illuminated the forms of two men, one seated on a barrel, the other standing. The man standing held a flashlight. The seated man held a pistol dangling from his right hand and what seemed to be a sheet of paper, illuminated by the flash, in the other. The seated man ignored the light from Chee's flash. The standing man looked into the flashlight. Joe Leaphorn.

"Wiley Denton," Chee shouted. "Drop the pistol."

Denton seemed not to hear.

"Police," Chee shouted. "Drop that pistol."

Chee had his own pistol cocked. He was aware of Bernie standing beside him.

Denton stood up, faced Chee, his pistol came up.

Chee leaped against Bernie, knocked her out of the doorway. His momentum slammed him into the doorjamb, the flashlight fell from his numbed arm. He found himself on his knees, still gripping his own pistol.

In the bunker he saw Denton standing, illuminated by Leaphorn's flashlight. No pistol visible now.

"He's all right," Leaphorn shouted. "Come on in."

Chee walked down the floor, pistol pointed. Bernie had recovered his flashlight and was walking with him, the light focused on Denton.

"Wiley," Leaphorn said. "Hand your pistol over to Sergeant Chee. You don't need it now."

Denton pulled the pistol out of the waistband of his trousers. "Take it," he said, and handed it to Chee.

"And the letter," Leaphorn said. "Let me keep that for you. You'll always want it."

Denton handed Leaphorn the letter, turned away from Chee, and put his arms behind his back.

"Mr. Denton," Chee said. "I arrest you for the murder of Thomas Doherty. You have the right to remain silent. You have the right to an attorney. Anything you say may be used against you."

"Oh!" Bernie exclaimed. "What did you do to your arm? It's bleeding."

"Banged it on the doorjamb," Chee said. "I'll take Mr. Denton out to the car and call this in." He was looking at Linda on her cardboard resting place. "Send an ambulance, I guess." He tugged at Denton's sleeve.

"Just a minute," Denton said, and turned to Leaphorn. "Let me read that last part again."

Leaphorn looked at Denton's hands, cuffed behind his back, said: "I'll read it to you."

"No. You don't need to do that," Denton said. "I can remember every word of it."

In the reflected light of the flash, Leaphorn's face looked old and exhausted. "Wiley," he said, "remember something else, too. Remember you didn't want this to happen. Remember this was because of a lot of misunderstanding."

"I'm remembering something else, too. That remark you made to me about Shakespeare. I asked the woman at the library about *Othello*, and she got me a copy. He was just about as stupid as me. But with me, I didn't have someone egging me on. I did it to myself. Looking for a treasure when I already had one."

"Come on," Chee said, and he and Wiley walked through the darkness toward the brilliant sunlight of the open door.

Bernie had been staring down at the body. She shook her head and turned away. "It's hard to believe this," she said. "She starved to death here in the dark. It's just too awful. What was McKay doing? Using her as a hostage, I guess. But why didn't Mr. Denton come and get her? What happened?"

"Denton shot McKay before he had time to tell him where he was holding Linda. Denton said he didn't believe any of it," Leaphorn said. "Don't you think we should get out of here?"

"What did Linda say?" Bernie asked, pointing to the paper in Leaphorn's hand. "Could I read it?"

Leaphorn didn't answer that.

"I guess not," she said. "But could you tell me whether she was angry?"

"I guess you would say it was a love letter," Leaphorn said. "She apologized for introducing McKay to Denton, said she didn't know McKay was an evil man. She said that since

Denton hadn't come for her, she was afraid McKay had killed him, and he would never then be able to read her letter. But she would slip off into dreams now and then, and she would dream of Denton being in a hospital, recovering. If he did, she knew he would come and she would try to stay alive until then. And if she failed him again, she wanted him to know that she always loved him and that she was sorry."

Leaphorn turned off the flashlight. He didn't want to see Bernie's face.

"She was sorry," Bernie said in a choked voice. "She said *she* was sorry?"

The reflected light from the doorway showed Leaphorn that Bernie's eyes were wet. Time to change the subject.

"What happened to Jim's arm?"

"Oh," she said. "When he saw Denton holding that pistol, he jumped into me. He knocked me out of the doorway."

"Hurt you?"

"No, it didn't hurt me," Bernie said, her tone indignant. "He was trying to protect me."

"I think we need to get out into the sunshine," Leaphorn said.

"I should stay," Bernie said. "I'm on duty.

Stay with the body until the crime scene crew gets here."

"I'll stay with you then," Leaphorn said. "Aren't you concerned about the *chindi*? Linda's ghost would have been locked in here with no way out."

"Lieutenant Leaphorn," Bernie said. "Haven't you forgotten? When one dies, their good goes with them. Only the bad is left behind to form the ghost. I doubt if Linda Denton left much of a *chindi*."

They stood beside the body for a while, with nothing to say. Bernie focused her flash on a little black plastic case partly obscured by Linda Denton's skirt and glanced at Leaphorn—a questioning look.

"That's some sort of miniature disc player," Leaphorn said. "She loved music, and Denton had just given it to her. Birthday present, I think he said."

"I guess that was the source of the music those kids heard. If it hadn't been for the wind wailing that night—" With that Bernie found a tissue in her pocket and wiped her eyes. "Hadn't been for the wind they would have known they were hearing Linda and not a ghost."

Leaphorn nodded. "We have that story of our own, you know, about the Hard Flint boys twisting the good air into evil."

"Right now I'm thinking my mother was right," she said. "There's just too much evil in this business for me. Too much sorrow."

"You wouldn't have any trouble getting another job," Leaphorn said. "Something where you help people instead of arresting them."

"I know," Bernie said. "I'm thinking about it. I'm going to quit this. I'd like to make people happy."

Leaphorn pointed toward the bunker door. Through it, they could see Sergeant Jim Chee putting Wiley Denton in his patrol car. "You know, Bernie, you could start that 'making people happy' career right now. Tell that young man out there what you've just told me."

Bernie looked out into the sunlight, at Chee talking to Denton through the car window. She looked back at Leaphorn, shrugged, spread her hands in that gesture of defeated frustration.

Leaphorn nodded. "I know," he said. "When I was a lot younger, an old Zuñi told me their legend about that. Two of their young hunters rescued a dragonfly stuck in the mud. It gave them the usual wishes you get in these stories. One wished to be the smartest man in the world. The dragonfly said, 'So you shall be.' But the second hunter wanted to be smarter than the smartest man in the world."

On this Leaphorn paused, partly for effect, partly to see if Bernie had already heard a version of this, and partly to see if she had cheered up enough to be listening. She was listening.

"So the dragonfly converted the second hunter into a woman," Bernie said, laughing and nodding at Leaphorn.

"I'm retired from the Navajo Tribal Police, but I'm still commissioned as a McKinley County deputy sheriff," he said. "I can stay here with the body."

Then he watched her walk toward the open door. Toward the dazzling sunlight. Toward Jim Chee.

As Tony's home state paper the *Oklahoma City Oklahoman* says, "Readers who have not discovered Hillerman should not waste one minute more." Find out what you've been missing with Leaphorn and Chee . . .

*A supernatural killer known as the "Wolf-Witch" be-
comes Leaphorn's target on a thrilling mystic pur-
suit.*

THE BLESSING WAY

When Lt. Joe Leaphorn of the Navajo Tribal Police dis-
covers a corpse with a mouth full of sand at a crime
scene seemingly without tracks or clues, he is ready to
suspect a supernatural killer. Blood on the rocks . . . A
body on the high mesa . . . Leaphorn must stalk the
Wolf-Witch along a chilling trail between mysticism
and murder.

"A thriller . . . Highly recommended."
The New Yorker

"Brilliant . . . As fascinating as it is original."
St. Louis Post-Dispatch

A dead reporter's secret notebook implicates a senatorial candidate and political figures in a million-dollar murder scam.

THE FLY ON THE WALL

John Cotton was a simple man with one desire: to write the greatest story of his life and have enough life left to read all about it. He knows what to do when he finds a great story, but he is a little afraid when a big story begins to find him. It starts when a fellow reporter is murdered and his notebook, filled with information about a tax scam, ends up in John's hands. Not long afterwards, a body is discovered in John's car. Then John's car ends up in the river, a bomb is found in his apartment, and his girlfriend drops out of sight. It's up to John to unravel the mystery of the notebook and why anyone would kill for the information it contains.

"Fascinating . . . breathless suspense."
The Minneapolis Tribune

"Explosive . . . sensational . . . excellent."
The Cleveland Plain Dealer

An archaeological dig, a steel hypodermic needle, and the strange laws of the Zuñi complicate the disappearance of two young boys.

DANCE HALL OF THE DEAD

Two young boys suddenly disappear. One of them, a Zuñi, leaves a pool of blood behind. Lt. Joe Leaphorn of the Navajo Tribal Police tracks the brutal killer. Three things complicate the search: an archeological dig, a steel hypodermic needle, and the strange laws of the Zuñi. Compelling, terrifying, and highly suspenseful, *Dance Hall of the Dead* never relents from first page till last.

"High entertainment, an aesthetically satisfying glimpse of the still-powerful tribal mysteries."
The New York Times

Riveting descriptions of Zuñi rites

A baffling investigation of murder, ghosts, and witches can be solved only by Lt. Leaphorn, a man who understands both his own people and cold-blooded killers.

LISTENING WOMAN

The state police and FBI are baffled when an old man and a teenage girl are brutally murdered. The blind Navajo Listening Woman speaks of ghosts and of witches. But Lieutenant Leaphorn of the Navajo Tribal Police knows his people as well as he knows cold-blooded killers. His incredible investigation carries him from a dead man's secret to a kidnap scheme, to a conspiracy that stretches back more than one hundred years. Leaphorn arrives at the threshold of a solution—and is greeted with the most violent confrontation of his career.

"Hillerman's mysteries are special . . . *Listening Woman* is among the best."
Washington Post

"A good exciting mystery that has everything."
Pittsburgh Press

An assassin waits for Officer Chee in the desert to protect a vision of death that for thirty years has been fed by greed and washed by blood.

PEOPLE OF DARKNESS

Who would murder a dying man? Why would someone steal a box of rocks? And why would a rich man's wife pay $3,000 to get them back? These questions haunt Sgt. Jim Chee of the Navajo Tribal Police as he journeys into the scorching Southwest. But there, out in the Bad Country, a lone assassin waits for Chee to come seeking answers, waits ready and willing to protect a vision of death that for thirty years has been fed by greed and washed in blood.

"Hillerman . . . is in a class by himself."
Los Angeles Times

"Great suspense."
Chicago Tribune

Sgt. Jim Chee becomes trapped in a deadly web of a cunningly spun plot driven by Navajo sorcery and white man's greed.

THE DARK WIND

A corpse whose palms and soles have been "scalped" is only the first in a series of disturbing clues: an airplane's mysterious crash in the nighttime desert, a bizarre attack on a windmill, a vanishing shipment of cocaine. Sgt. Jim Chee of the Navajo Tribal Police is trapped in the deadly web of a cunningly spun plot driven by Navajo sorcery and white man's greed.

"Hillerman is first-rate . . . fresh, original, and highly suspenseful."
Los Angeles Times

"A beauty of a thriller . . . exotic and compelling reading."
Cleveland Plain Dealer

A photo sends Officer Chee on an odyssey of murder and revenge that moves from an Indian hogan to a deadly healing ceremony.

THE GHOSTWAY

Old Joseph Joe sees it all. Two strangers spill blood at the Shiprock Wash-O-Mat. One dies. The other drives off into the dry lands of the Big Reservation, but not before he shows the old Navajo a photo of the man he seeks. This is enough to send Tribal Policeman Jim Chee after a killer . . . and on an odyssey of murder and revenge that moves from an Indian hogan and its trapped ghost, to the dark underbelly of L.A., to a healing ceremony whose cure could be death.

"A first-rate story of suspense and mystery."
The New Yorker

"Fresh, original and highly suspenseful."
Los Angeles Times

Three shotgun blasts in a trailer bring Officer Chee and Lt. Leaphorn together for the first time in an investigation of ritual, witchcraft, and blood.

SKINWALKERS

Three shotgun blasts explode into the trailer of Officer Jim Chee of the Navajo Tribal Police. But Chee survives to join partner Lt. Joe Leaphorn in a frightening investigation that takes them into a dark world of ritual, witchcraft, and blood — all tied to the elusive and evil "skinwalker." Brimming with Navajo lore and sizzling suspense, *Skinwalkers* brings Chee and Leaphorn, Hillerman's best-selling detective team, together for the first time.

"Full of mystery, intrigue, and
dangerous magic."
Ross Thomas

"Hillerman is unique and *Skinwalkers*
is one of his best."
Los Angeles Times

Stolen ancient goods and new corpses at an ancient burial site confound Leaphorn and Chee. They must plunge into the past to unearth the truth.

A THIEF OF TIME

A noted anthropologist vanishes at a moonlit Indian ruin where "thieves of time" ravage sacred ground for profit. When two corpses appear amid stolen goods and bones at an ancient burial site, Navajo Tribal Policemen Lt. Joe Leaphorn and Officer Jim Chee must plunge into the past to unearth the astonishing truth behind a mystifying series of horrific murders.

"Skillful. Provocative. The action never flags."
New York Times Book Review

"Vintage Tony Hillerman: suspenseful, compelling! Hillerman transcends the mystery genre and this is one of [his] best."
Washington Post Book World

A grave robber and a corpse reunite Leaphorn and Chee in a dangerous arena of superstition, ancient ceremony, and living gods.

TALKING GOD

As Leaphorn seeks the identity of a murder victim, Chee is arresting Smithsonian conservator Henry Highhawk for ransacking the sacred bones of his ancestors. As the layers of each case are peeled away, it becomes shockingly clear that they are connected, that there are mysterious others pursuing Highhawk, and that Leaphorn and Chee have entered into the dangerous arena of superstition, ancient ceremony, and living gods.

"Woven as tightly as a Navajo blanket."
Newsweek

"Suddenly now Hillerman has become a national literary and cultural sensation . . . it does not take too much to determine why Hillerman has become so popular. He is a solid, down-to-earth storyteller."
Los Angeles Times

When a bullet kills Officer Jim Chee's good friend Del, a Navajo shaman is arrested for homicide, but the case is far from closed.

COYOTE WAITS

The car fire didn't kill Navajo Tribal Policeman Delbert Nez, a bullet did. Officer Jim Chee's good friend Del lies dead, and a whiskey-soaked Navajo shaman is found with the murder weapon. The old man is Ashie Pinto. He's quickly arrested for homicide and defended by a woman Chee could either love or loathe. But when Pinto won't utter a word of confession or denial, Lt. Joe Leaphorn begins an investigation. Soon, Leaphorn and Chee unravel a complex plot of death involving an historical find, a lost fortune . . . and the mythical Coyote, who is always waiting, and always hungry.

"Hillerman is at the top of his form in
Coyote Waits."
San Francisco Chronicle

"The master's newest Chee-Leaphorn
mystery with the usual informative Navajo
anthropology."
Book News

Officer Chee attempts to solve two modern murders by deciphering the sacred clown's ancient message to the people of the Tano pueblo.

SACRED CLOWNS

During a Tano kachina ceremony something in the antics of the dancing *koshare* fills the air with tension. Moments later the clown is found brutally bludgeoned in the same manner that a reservation schoolteacher was killed just days before.

In true Navajo style, Officer Jim Chee and Lieutenant Leaphorn of the Navajo Tribal Police go back to the beginning to decipher the sacred clowns' message to the people of the Tano pueblo. Amid guarded tribal secrets and crooked Indian traders, they find a trail of blood that links a runaway schoolboy, two dead bodies, and the mysterious presence of a sacred artifact.

"This is Hillerman at his best, mixing human nature, ethnicity and the overpowering physical presence of the Southwest."
Newsweek

"[Hillerman's] affection for his characters and for the real world in which they live and work has never been more appealingly demonstrated."
Los Angeles Times Book Review

A man met his death on Ship Rock Mountain eleven years ago, and with the discovery of his body by a group of climbers, Chee and Leaphorn must hunt down the cause of his lonely death.

FALLEN MAN

Sprawled on a ledge under the peak of Ship Rock Mountain for eleven years lies an unknown body, now only bones. At Canyon de Chelly, three hundred miles across the Navajo reservation, a sniper shoots an old canyon guide who has always walked that pollen path in peace. At his home in Window Rock, Joe Leaphorn, newly retired from the Navajo Tribal Police, connects skeleton and sniper, and remembers an old puzzle he could never solve. At his office in Shiprock, Acting Lieutenant Jim Chee is too busy to take much interest in the case—until it hits too close to home. Bringing the beauty and mystery of the Southwest to vivid life once again, Tony Hillerman has reunited Joe Leaphorn and Jim Chee in an evocative mystery in which the past and the present join forces in a most unholy union.

> "The personal tensions add another facet
> to the story, which continues the author's
> fascination with the savagery that men
> do to themselves and to the land they claim to
> hold sacred."
> *New York Times Book Review*

THE WAILING WIND

"Hillerman's legion of fans . . . will likely
find it irresistible."
Kirkus Reviews

When Acting Lt. Jim Chee catches a Hopi poacher huddled over a butchered Navajo Tribal Police officer, he has an open-and-shut case—until his former boss, Joe Leaphorn, blows it wide open.

FIRST EAGLE

Now retired from the Navajo Tribal Police, Leaphorn has been hired to find a hot-headed female biologist hunting for the key to a virulent plague lurking in the Southwest. The scientist disappeared from the same area the same day the Navajo cop was murdered. Is she a suspect or another victim? And what about a report that a skinwalker—a Navajo witch—was seen at the same time and place too? For Leaphorn and Chee, the answers lie buried in a complicated knot of superstition and science, in a place where the worlds of native peoples and outside forces converge and collide.

"Surrendering to Hillerman's strong narrative voice and supple storytelling techniques, we come to see that ancient cultures and modern sciences are simply different mythologies for the same reality."
New York Times Book Review

"Hillerman's trademark melding of Navajo tradition and modern culture is captured with crystal clarity in this tale of an ancient

scourge's resurgence in today's world.
The uneasy mix of old ways and new is
articulated with resonant depth..."
Publishers Weekly

Hunting Badger *finds Navajo Tribal Police officers Joe Leaphorn and Jim Chee working two angles of the same case—each trying to catch the right-wing militiamen who pulled off a violent heist at an Indian casino.*

HUNTING BADGER

Three armed men raid the Ute tribe's gambling casino, and then disappear in the maze of canyons on the Utah-Arizona border. The FBI takes over the investigation, and agents swarm in with helicopters and high-tech equipment. Making an explosive situation even hotter, these experts devise a theory of the crime that makes a wounded deputy sheriff a suspect — a development that brings in Tribal Police Sergeant Jim Chee and his longtime colleague, retired Lieutenant Joe Leaphorn, to help.

Chee finds a fatal flaw in the federal theory and Leaphorn sees an intriguing pattern connecting this crime with the exploits of a legendary Ute hero bandit. Balancing politics, outsiders, and missing armed fugitives, Leaphorn and Chee soon find themselves caught in the most perplexing—and deadly—crime hunt of their lives...

"Hillerman soars."
Boston Globe

"Hillerman continues to dazzle . . . A standout."
Washington Post Book World